"Please..." Bunny framed shakily. "...the ring."

Sebastian set the tiny box on the table. Bunny's eyes were stinging, pain and guilt and a whole host of other emotions swimming around inside her and threatening to spill over into the tears that were all too ready to assail her in recent times. She didn't need a doctor to tell her that her hormones were all roaring into pregnancy hyperdrive.

The ring was a glorious glittering diamond surrounded by emeralds in an art deco geometric shape. "It's gorgeous," she whispered admiringly.

"Did I say something wrong?" Sebastian demanded in a raw undertone.

"Sit down," Bunny urged. "I get dizzy when you stand over me."

Lean bronzed profile taut, Sebastian sat back down in his seat.

Bunny leaned forward and immediately reached for both of his hands. "You *know* that you don't really want to marry me—"

"I beg your pardon," Sebastian challenged, sculpted jaw determined.

Lynne Graham was born in Northern Ireland and has been a keen romance reader since her teens. She is very happily married to an understanding husband who has learned to cook since she started to write! Her five children keep her on her toes. She has a very large dog who knocks everything over, a very small terrier who barks a lot and two cats. When time allows, Lynne is a keen gardener.

Books by Lynne Graham

Harlequin Presents

The Italian's Bride Worth Billions
The Baby the Desert King Must Claim
Two Secrets to Shock the Italian
His Royal Bride Replacement

Cinderella Sisters for Billionaires

The Maid Married to the Billionaire
The Maid's Pregnancy Bombshell

The Diamond Club

Baby Worth Billions

The Diamandis Heirs

Greek's Shotgun Wedding
Greek's One-Night Babies

Visit the Author Profile page
at Harlequin.com for more titles.

SHOCK GREEK HEIR

LYNNE GRAHAM

PRESENTS

If you purchased this book without a cover you should be aware that this book is stolen property. It was reported as "unsold and destroyed" to the publisher, and neither the author nor the publisher has received any payment for this "stripped book."

Recycling programs for this product may not exist in your area.

ISBN-13: 978-1-335-21317-4

Shock Greek Heir

Copyright © 2025 by Lynne Graham

All rights reserved. No part of this book may be used or reproduced in any manner whatsoever without written permission.

Without limiting the author's and publisher's exclusive rights, any unauthorized use of this publication to train generative artificial intelligence (AI) technologies is expressly prohibited.

This is a work of fiction. Names, characters, places and incidents are either the product of the author's imagination or are used fictitiously. Any resemblance to actual persons, living or dead, businesses, companies, events or locales is entirely coincidental.

For questions and comments about the quality of this book, please contact us at CustomerService@Harlequin.com.

TM and ® are trademarks of Harlequin Enterprises ULC.

 Harlequin Enterprises ULC
22 Adelaide St. West, 41st Floor
Toronto, Ontario M5H 4E3, Canada
www.Harlequin.com

Printed in Lithuania

MIX
Paper | Supporting responsible forestry
www.fsc.org FSC® C021394

SHOCK GREEK HEIR

With warmest love and thanks to my daughter, Rachel,
my port in every storm

CHAPTER ONE

SEBASTIAN PAGONIS, TECH BILLIONAIRE, vaulted out of his helicopter on the Indonesian island. His big, powerful body sheathed in chinos and a khaki shirt, dwarfed everyone around him by virtue of his six-foot, five-inch height. His shock of black hair was anchored in a messy man bun, thin steel rings glinted in both earlobes, and he turned heads wherever he went because he looked so downright dangerous.

Glittering dark eyes that gleamed like polished swords in the sunshine scanned his surroundings with vigilance and he was greeted in the shadow of the hangar by an old schoolfriend, Andreas Zervas, who ran the Asian manufacturing side of his business. Andreas, his short, somewhat rounded counterpart, in a light summer suit, grinned up at him with familiar warmth.

'I intended to meet you off your jet in Bali but our newborn ignored etiquette and arrived early and suddenly. Why right now do you look as if you're expecting a hitman to be hiding in the shadows?'

'That would literally be the *only* option my relatives haven't yet attempted,' Sebastian retorted in frank exasperation.

Andreas frowned because he knew exactly what his friend was talking about.

Sebastian's paternal grandmother, Loukia Pagonis had died some weeks earlier and her last will and testament had given her family, including Sebastian, a resounding shock. Without any warning, she had made Sebastian, the outcast in the Pagonis tribe and a man already rich beyond avarice, the heir to her vast international property empire. Ever since then, Sebastian had been fighting off lawsuits and enraged and embittered accusations. The family who had long treated him like a curse on their name and an intolerable social embarrassment were currently reaping the rewards of having treated him like a leper throughout his childhood.

'Don't joke about it,' Andreas reproved, an unusual frown on his good-natured face. 'Stranger things have happened and when you're planning a week off-grid without security, it makes my blood run cold.'

'It's a week off and I...*need* it,' Sebastian admitted grudgingly, intense fatigue briefly bowing his broad shoulders and weighting his dark, deep voice. 'Did you make the final arrangements?'

Andreas sighed as he escorted him towards a top-of-the-range SUV. 'I did but I still think it's a crazy idea. You can't go back. You think you can but you *can't*. You're not that seventeen-year-old boy without a home any more. You're not used to roughing it now either. This experience will be a penance for you, which is why I'm breaking your rules and giving you a burner phone to take with you. You'll be screaming for escape within forty-eight hours. Your nature is too driven not to be and you'll be pining for your superyacht even quicker. It isn't easy to move from the fast lane to the slow sailing life.'

'I have to adapt for the sake of my sanity,' Sebastian growled, irritated by that negative forecast from someone who knew him well. 'But I'll take the phone if it makes you worry less...as long as yours is the only number in it.'

'It is,' Andreas confirmed, taking the wheel to drive them out of the private airfield and down a rural road edged by paddy fields contained by low walls. The car entered a small village to thread slowly through narrow, crowded streets with dust flying up to cloud the windscreen. From there they drew into a small, shabby harbour.

'Give my love to Zoe and the children. What gender is the newborn? You still haven't told me—'

'A little girl after our three boys. We are both over the moon,' Andreas told him happily.

'I'll stop in for the night on my way back next week,' Sebastian promised as he gathered his stuff.

'Look after yourself...and try to be a good loser

when you're climbing the walls to get back on shore by tomorrow,' Andreas quipped.

'It's not going to happen,' Sebastian asserted with amusement.

'So, who is this guy, Sebastian Whatever-You-Call-Him?' Bunny asked the skipper of the catamaran *Merry Days*.

For the past month, she had been crewing for Reggie, taking daily parties of tourists out to sail round the islands, serving drinks and providing lunch.

Sadly, however, Indonesia was the very last stop on her world travels. She had neither the time nor the money to explore further. Whether she liked it or not, home was beckoning. In just two weeks, she would be starting work back in the UK as a librarian and that was her cue to settle down and concentrate on her career.

Reggie Davis grinned above his imposing long white beard, bright blue eyes sparkling with satisfaction. 'He's Greek born. According to my source he's also *filthy* rich but prefers to be treated like he's ordinary, for goodness' sake. I mean, can you believe that? I'm giving him my cabin because it's more private and I don't think he'll want to be eating with us, so I'm afraid you'll have to serve him his meals.'

'How does that come under the heading of treating him like he's ordinary?'

'Reckon he's one of those odd, reserved types with quirks because who would hire the whole boat sooner than have to share the facilities?' Reggie asked in wonderment, being a man who had never met anyone he couldn't make into a friend and who flourished best in a crowd. 'But what do we care? Take him sailing, diving, fishing, snorkelling, whatever he wants...mostly just a taste of freedom, I suppose.'

'I'd better get your cabin cleared out,' Bunny said abruptly. 'And maybe I should go to the market.'

'No, if he wants to be ordinary, he eats what we eat even if he does choose to eat alone,' Reggie decreed squarely. 'Nothing fancy, just the norm. He'll not be complaining when he's sitting with one of your curries in front of him.'

'Let's hope not,' Bunny agreed, already on her feet, a small, slightly built blonde with luminous green eyes set in a heart-shaped face and a deep tan from her travels over the past year. She was in her last job at her final destination and about to deal with her last customer. Why did that knowledge sadden her? She went topside to access Reggie's cabin behind the wheelhouse, scolding herself for being spoilt. After all, she had finally enjoyed the year of travel she had first craved when she was eighteen and had been denied.

Her family were naturally overprotective. She was the youngest of six and the only girl. As a result, she had been babied long beyond childhood. Her desire to travel alone for a year between school and university had horrified her family. Their preaching, nagging and genuine concern had finally talked her out of her plans and she had gone to university and completed her degree before taking her year out. In truth that had ended up being the better plan, she conceded, because she had spent four years saving up everything she earned in part-time jobs to finance her travels. She had also taken casual work in every country that allowed her to do so, ensuring that she had a safety net of cash available should she need it.

The next day, Bunny was down on her knees scrubbing the deck when their passenger arrived, the fast slap of his booted feet on the steps sending her head rearing up, fine blonde hair flying back from her face because she was hot and damp with perspiration in the humid afternoon heat.

Simply stunned by the vision of the man in front of her, she leant back and stared at the guy who had boarded. He was so off-the-scales magnificent that he might have stepped out of a Viking fantasy onscreen. Incredibly tall and broad, not to mention jaw-droppingly gorgeous. One look and her mouth ran dry and her brain seized up.

'Could you just give me two minutes until I finish the deck?' she asked breathlessly.

'No,' Sebastian responded succinctly as if he were still in his busy office. 'You're in a service industry and you should be aware that clients expect immediate attention.'

Even as her slender spine stiffened, Bunny smiled brightly at him. So, he was one of *those*, was he? Oh, joy, she thought, pained to the bone by that warning. 'Thank you for the reminder, sir. Please come this way...'

'Where's the skipper?' Sebastian scrutinised her, unimpressed. He had recognised the shellshocked, dazed look of feminine appreciation in her gaze for what it was and it had annoyed him. Not only had he not expected there to be a woman onboard, but he also didn't want her looking at him like *that*, flirting or hovering or aiming to impress. He got enough of that nonsense every day of the week and he wasn't about to put up with it on a tiny boat where there were few places to escape unwelcome attention. The sooner any such notion of hers was nipped in the bud, the better.

On the other hand, she was surprisingly attractive in a girl-next-door way even if she wasn't his type. Did he even have a type, though? She was naturally blonde, naturally everything he suspected. Cute little face, enormous green eyes the colour of fresh spring leaves, freckles on her small nose above a generous pink mouth. Ridiculously pretty but rather small and thin with modest curves. And cheeky, even if she was striving to hide the fact. Didn't she know yet that her eyes blazed green fire when she was angry?

'Skipper Reggie takes a nap mid-afternoon. I'm afraid I'm on service duty. I'll show you to your cabin.'

Awkwardly wiping her hands on the back of her denim shorts, Bunny offered to take his bag. He frowned, spectacular dark eyes hardening. 'Your hands are dirty.'

'Are you willing to wait while I wash them?'

'No, just lead the way. I'll retain my luggage,' Sebastian retorted curtly.

Charming, she thought grimly as she showed him to his cabin. It was the largest on board and benefited from private facilities but it was still pretty small and he was so very tall; he'd be lucky if he could stand upright any place but in the open air. Richie Rich, she labelled him, just dripping with condescension and gilded expectations that were unlikely to be met on a forty-odd-foot catamaran with a crew of two.

'We usually have dinner at seven. I'll bring it to you. Would you like a drink now or anything else?'

'Water, please,' he said flatly. '*And*...don't speak to me unless you have to.'

Bunny nodded in tight-mouthed silence, spun on her heel and left him to it while she went to fetch the cold water. She was a minion, she realised wryly, and minions were not supposed to have a voice that was heard. Returning with the bottle of chilled water, she knocked on the door. He answered with a towel wrapped round his impressively lean waist and she stepped back immediately from that intimacy. Confronted by a masculine torso that was undeniably centrefold material, she was uncomfortable and she extended the bottle in silence, not bothering to speak since he had already told her that speech from her corner was undesirable.

She went back down to the galley to make a start on dinner. She heard male voices, registering that Reggie had emerged from his nap and was getting acquainted with his passenger. Steps moved overhead as the catamaran moved sleekly through the water. Reggie came down and took a couple of beers out of the fridge.

'Sebastian's okay,' he told her cheerfully. 'Very down to earth, no front to him. We're getting on like a house on fire. Oh, remind me to post the change to our route. You'll enjoy it. We're heading somewhere rather remote and I haven't been there in a few years. There's a great fishing spot waiting for us. We'll definitely have the barbecue up on deck that night.'

Bunny kept on smiling. No front to him? *Sebastian?* She gritted her teeth and when it was time she took the men's meals up on deck and left them there to eat, discreetly ignoring Reggie's suggestion that she join them. As she ate alone, she listened to the distant chatter and the laughter and thought that possibly Sebastian just didn't like female crew members. Or maybe it was just *her*, *her* face, *her* personality, whatever, she thought, irritated that she was even thinking about such a thing. Life was too short for her to be that sensitive. What did it matter what a guy she would never see again thought of her? Everybody got on with Reggie though. Maybe she personally needed to work a little harder on that score, she thought next.

As usual she was up at dawn the next morning,

taking care of all the little jobs that were hers before making breakfast. By seven she was knocking on Sebastian's door with a tray.

'Come in!' he called.

One arm balancing the tray, with difficulty she got the door open and saw him sitting up bare-chested in the bed. Moving closer, her face hot at that amount of exposure to male nudity, she extended the tray to him. He grasped it one-handed, being better balanced and stronger than she was and then frowned down at the plate. 'What is this gloop?' he demanded.

'It's a Spanish omelette,' she told him curtly on the way back out. 'Reggie's favourite. It's always eggs for breakfast. If you prefer them prepared another way, let me know.'

'Scrambled, plain,' he specified.

In silence, Bunny nodded, her heart-shaped face flushed with annoyance, Sebastian noticed with growing amusement.

'How did you get a nickname like Bunny?' he asked out of sheer badness.

'My family thought it was cute when I was a baby. It's on my birth certificate,' Bunny admitted with a stiff and decidedly grudging smile before she withdrew.

Sebastian grinned. She hated him and she couldn't hide it... Mission accomplished: she would be staying out of his way all week. This was not the right moment to acknowledge that she had fabulous legs and a mouth made for, well, what a man usually hoped a woman's mouth was made for. There was just something surprisingly sexy about her modest curves and prim, quiet movements. That had to be why he had a hard-on. Determined not to think about that weird glitch in his libido, he tucked into his first Spanish omelette and was surprised by how good it was. Possibly he owed her an apology.

Would he admit that? Probably not. A woman who couldn't even give him a first glance without revealing her every reaction to him was not the kind of woman he bedded. Too young, too naïve, too...*soft*. And he didn't *ever* do soft. As he had once learned to his cost, he reflected grimly, decent and honest intentions didn't always win the best results. He had got burned, badly enough burned by Ariana to ensure that he never went near that type of woman again. If he was the kind of guy who believed in love, he might have felt differently, but Sebastian had never believed in love outside familial love. A parent could love a child, and a child could love a parent. While that might not have been his experience, he had seen enough of the world to accept that he had got the birth parents from hell.

Love between a man and a woman? Just *no*. He almost shuddered in disgust at the thought of being caught up in such a lie, such a cruel fabrication, coined to cover greed, lust, infidelity and ambition, all of which he had witnessed within his own *un-*family circles. He wasn't likely to ever be the kind of idiot who fell for that love fantasy with a woman.

He was stronger than that, he knew better. He would be alone on his deathbed. Alone, he functioned better. Alone, he was happiest, hence his current solo voyage. When a woman asked him if he was a commitment-phobe, he just laughed because he was something worse than that. He had never *needed* anyone else in his life, not even as a child, and he could not imagine ever wanting a woman beside him for anything other than occasional sex.

Having eaten and set the world to rights inside his head, Sebastian sprang out of bed and went for a shower. True, the boat was tiny, there was a woman on it and he kept on bashing his head on ceilings and in doorways not intended for anyone of his height, but Reggie had promised to share his favourite fishing spot with him today and Sebastian was looking forward to kicking back with a beer, a rod and good company. Something that reminded him of a long-lost past, something so far removed from his usual daily schedule that it beckoned like an idyllic dream...

Bunny cleaned the galley, wondering how that oversized jerk on deck could imagine it was possible for her to provide more elaborate meals or choices in the minuscule space. When they took out a party of tourists, there was one basic lunch and that was that. She was no cordon bleu cook anyway. *Gloop?* And just assuming that Bunny was a nickname? Even though loads of people before Sebastian had assumed the same, she had got more than the drift of his meaning.

It *was* a horribly silly name and she had always been aware of it, even though her wretched family still rejoiced in it to the extent that it hadn't seemed worth the hassle of renaming herself for university as she had once intended. How would she ever have brought friends home who knew her by another name? And, of course, she had brought friends home, even though she hadn't wanted to, even though she would have loved to keep her new student life separate from her family. Finally, something for her and a little privacy, she had fondly believed.

But parents and big brothers who loved you interfered, needed to know, needed to be assured you were safe and she had gradually appreciated that that was the trade-off for all that love. And her family was always going to be like that, up there to their armpits in *her* business. At uni, however, she had met enough other people from less stable and caring families and had slowly learned the lesson that she had been lucky, luckier than she had ever realised with her nearest and dearest. Those from dysfunctional backgrounds could take out their pain on you if you weren't careful to avoid them, she conceded, her flushed face shadowing with bad memories she rarely took out. And she betted there was a bucketful of bad stuff behind Richie Rich with his Viking good looks and cold arrogance. He and she were complete opposites. Bunny liked everybody until they gave her reason to doubt them. Sebastian, it seemed, disliked them on sight.

Only not, clearly, Reggie, she acknowledged later that day, topping up the cool box with beers while the two men laughed and yarned over lazily dangling fishing rods. She was disconcerted, not having expected their passenger to be quite so relaxed with her boss. After all, there was nothing the least refined about Reggie, a hardworking seaman on the brink of retirement and at least twice Sebastian's age. Had she misjudged him? Was it a clash of personalities? Had she said some triggering word that had set him off to be unpleasant? And why was it *still* bothering her? He was some foreign rich guy, whom she would never see again after his week onboard ended.

Sebastian's gaze lingered on Bunny's struggle to cart up and organise a large barbecue. Every fibre of his being urged him to get up and help and his lean brown hands tightened into fists as he resisted the urge to behave like the gentleman he had been raised to be, but which he *wasn't* in any shape or form. Any attention at all fed women of her ilk and encouraged them. True, she hadn't looked even sidewise at him since he had warned her off and he couldn't understand why that heartening reality was now setting his teeth on edge. It was as if there were a blank space where he was. She didn't look, she didn't speak, she didn't even hang around when her boss tried to engage her.

'She'd shout at you if you tried to help,' Reggie told him without warning.

'Sorry?' For an instant, Sebastian was bewildered by that advice.

'Saw you look at Bunny struggling with the barbecue and feel bad, just warning you she'd bite your nose off if she thought you were treating her as less than a man in the same job. She's very tough and independent, not surprising with five brothers and an adoring family always round her,' Reggie mused absently, stretching back into his comfy old seat on deck and reaching for his beer again. 'Her mother is still sending her *care* packages every week even though she's on the other side of the world. I'm scared to tell her that every week her father or one of her brothers calls me checking that she's all right. They're smothering her alive and she's a good kid, hardworking, friendly, everything you could want on a boat like this...it's a shame.'

Sebastian did not respond because he was a sympathy-free zone, having no experience whatsoever of family fussing over him, not a one of them, even Loukia, whom he had loved. Too late had his grandmother realised what his childhood had been like and he could only assume that guilt had influenced her groundbreaking decision not to challenge the trust set up by his grandfather, guilt that she hadn't taken Sebastian in personally rather than palming him off on other family members. No doubt that was why he was now even richer than he had ever desired to be.

In his opinion, however, Reggie's little spiel only warned him that Bunny was spoilt and likely a brat if there was the remotest chance of her being rude to a customer or her boss. But even while he was thinking that he was closely watching every move she made as she squatted down to try again to level the legs of the barbecue, bent over it, peachy bottom flexing, plump breasts bouncing under her tee shirt. Not an ounce of fat on her except where a man wanted it, he noted, his zip tightening yet again across his groin.

His reaction infuriated him. There was just something strange about her that attracted him and, of course, he wasn't about to do anything about it, even as he saw the way the sunlight burnished her streaky blonde hair, the delicacy of her profile, the almost fairy-tale points of her ears. And what about what he was now *convinced* was the far from innocent stretching and bending and flexing of that erotic body in his presence? A simple display of the goods, he reckoned impatiently.

'How do your male customers take to her?' Sebastian enquired silkily.

Reggie dealt him a startled glance. 'Well, they *don't*, if you know what I mean. She doesn't encourage that kind of thing. She's a black belt in judo, as one of my over-friendly customers discovered last month. He was flat on his back and stuttering apologies by the time I came on them. Stupid drunk...!' the older man completed, using some Indonesian word that evidently hit the spot for him but which Sebastian, who spoke several languages, didn't recognise.

'I reckon she's too challenging for most young blokes...and then you've got her family to get past into the bargain,' Reggie remarked, vaulting upright with lean vigour and crossing the deck to take charge of levelling the barbecue while Bunny stood by with folded arms and a stubborn, irritated look on her face.

Too challenging? Sebastian concealed a smile, thinking that all he would have to do was snap his fingers and she'd drop into his hands like a ripe peach. Only he wasn't thinking of doing that, was he? No way was he ruining his week off with any of that nonsense! Sex was always available to him wherever he was in the world. In any case, he had made her hate him now and it would require effort to lure her back and he never, ever made an effort with women because that only encouraged their delusions of being important to him. No, Sebastian had tried-and-trusted methods of handling women and he wasn't planning to go off-piste any time soon.

Why the hell was that jerk always watching her? Bunny frowned down at the sizzling fish on the grill and swallowed hard. She was hot and she was tired because she had worked a long day. She shovelled her own meal on a plate and set it aside before carrying the men's plates over to the table already furnished with a bowl of salad, quinoa laced with Indonesian spices and the fresh bread she baked every day.

'You're not joining us *again*?' Reggie queried in surprise as she walked away with her own plate.

'No. Got a book waiting on me and maybe a swim afterwards,' she muttered, shooting a reluctant glance back even as Sebastian, utter hypocrite that he was, pulled out the third chair at the table as if keen to welcome her.

She went down to the galley, which was even hotter and more airless, and ate with more haste than enjoyment. Then she remembered that she hadn't changed the jerk's bed or his towels and she sped back on deck to cover that necessity.

His cabin was a tip of discarded clothes. Did he have servants who usually picked up after him? She tidied up as best she could, gathering up an impossibly soft fancy sweater in beige and noticing that the label was Dior, momentarily drawing it to her cheek just to feel that incredible softness against her skin. It was probably cashmere and cost more than she had ever earned in a single year. The ridiculously evocative scent of his skin, citrusy, earthy, *sexy*, engulfed her. He smelled incredibly good.

Guiltily, she folded the garment up and put it back where she had found it, not wishing to be accused of snooping. She replaced the towels and cleaned the little bathroom quickly and efficiently, eager to escape even while she wondered why she had sniffed his jumper like some addict. She was embarrassed by that prompting and still questioning it when she emerged from the cabin again and ran slap bang into its occupant.

'Bunny...what were you—?'

'Cleaning and changing the linen. My job,' Bunny told him with a fixed smile.

Actually, he hadn't been challenging what she had been doing in his cabin. 'I don't need frills on this trip,' he told her, faint colour darkening his high cheekbones as he met green eyes cold as charity and conceded that he might have gone a little overboard in his determination to keep her at a distance.

'Changing beds and cleaning is the norm on this boat, sir. Usually there are six to eight passengers to look after, so one is nothing.'

'But you're already doing all the cooking...and other stuff,' Sebastian reasoned, wondering why he was even talking to her, wondering why he sounded as though he was trying to apologise when he was a man who would require torture before admitting to being in the wrong. He had done too much apologising as a kid and an adolescent, striving to meet the expectations of others. Back then he had been too naïve to see that the combination of his great wealth and his sky-high IQ simply rubbed people up the wrong way. With his horrendous background and experiences, those same people had happily expected him to be a loser, a whiner and a waste of space and had thoroughly disliked him for becoming a winner instead.

'That is my job...sir,' Bunny added curtly.

Sebastian folded his arms. 'I think we got off on the wrong foot. When I asked you not to speak to me, I didn't mean that I wanted you to isolate yourself on a boat this size!'

'No problem, sir,' Bunny said woodenly, hating him with such a passion that it was a marvel he didn't spontaneously combust in front of her. He didn't know what he wanted from her, service or normal, friendly assistance, but he had been super quick and keen to banish any prospect of normality.

'You're being oversensitive,' Sebastian informed her, stormy dark eyes flashing gold. 'I'm trying to say that you don't need to keep your distance from me. That day, I was in a mood.'

'Perhaps I prefer to keep my distance from you.' Bunny was getting madder and madder behind her set smile.

'No,' Sebastian contradicted with crisp bite. 'If you hadn't made it so obvious that you found me attractive when I arrived, I would never have reacted as I did. The initial fault was *yours*, not mine.'

CHAPTER TWO

BUNNY'S JAW DROPPED because she couldn't honestly credit that he had said that to her face. Or that he could be so shamelessly confident of his undeniably spectacular dark good looks that he flung it in her teeth full force to shame her.

Stunned green eyes lifted to his face. 'You're not a very nice person.'

'No, I'm not,' Sebastian agreed in a driven undertone, questioning exactly how, when he had approached her in an attempt to make amends, he had ended up losing his temper with her instead and giving her the facts as he saw them.

Bunny gritted her teeth because lying did not come easily to her. 'I do *not* find you attractive… except to look at,' she declared with gathering steam. 'Your personality is seriously wanting on several fronts.'

Sebastian was incensed beyond belief at that condemnation. No woman had ever talked to him like that. She was rude, offensive and…and without warning he was burning for the chance to snatch her off her feet and plonk her down unceremoniously on his cabin bed and prove that personality had nothing whatsoever to do with sexual chemistry. *That*, they had in spades, he conceded, hooded dark eyes keenly raking her flushed and furious face.

'Liar,' he chided softly with his slow-burning rarely seen smile.

Bunny's small face froze and paled as though he had slapped her. For a split second that dazzling smile of his unleashed butterflies in her stomach. She wanted to tell him that he was a four-letter word of a person but she wasn't about to start swearing for his benefit. How could he say that? How could he be so *sure* that she had momentarily looked at him much as if a famous movie-screen star had unexpectedly stepped onboard? Of course he was sure, an inner voice piped up. He was drop-dead gorgeous and thoroughly aware of the fact. Arrogant, vain and self-satisfied—everything she hated in the opposite sex and she had to get stuck with him on a stupid boat!

'Excuse me,' she said stiffly, bending to bundle up the giant pile of laundry. 'I want to get in a swim before dark.'

Sebastian suppressed a groan. Bunny, it seemed, was not easily placated. 'Look, before you make your boss suspicious, start joining us for meals,' he urged with finality before he disappeared into the cabin.

In receipt of that unsought advice, Bunny breathed in, deep and slow, and went down to her own cabin to don her serviceable swimsuit. Minutes later, she was diving into the turquoise crystal-clear water, sunlight dappling the surface and almost blinding her. Soon enough the sun would be sinking and darkness would fold in. Maybe tomorrow she would consider communal meals, she reasoned absently, questioning why she would do that when she knew Reggie well enough to know that he would never question what she did in her free time.

From the far end of the boat, Sebastian watched her slicing through the water with the confidence of a mermaid, the fading light silvering every slender line of her body, accentuating her grace. A breeze whipped across the sea and she turned and headed back to the catamaran. She grabbed up a colourful towel and wrapped it round her, walking past the wheelhouse to say, 'Anyone want anything? Drinks? Snacks?'

Sebastian stood up and tugged out the spare chair for her. 'Join us for a drink,' he urged.

'Just feeling too sleepy tonight,' she said with her easy smile, the most natural smile she had ever given him. 'Maybe tomorrow.'

And something inside Sebastian flipped in reaction to those sparkling green eyes and the oddest feeling of disappointment. That weird sensation shook him and thoroughly alarmed him. He didn't know what to do with it or even what it was. She was a stranger, she wasn't his familiar type of glossy, glitzy woman. She was poor and he was rich and he didn't do Cinderella. He was also never likely to be any woman's prince.

Wide sensual mouth compressing, Sebastian sank back into his own seat. Reggie trimmed the sails on the mast, muttering about there being nothing on the weather about a storm but that, even if it was the wrong season for one, he felt happier taking precautions because the wind was still getting up. Sebastian rose to help because, when he was a teenager, he had spent two years sailing a catamaran of his own. That was when he had come to terms with who he was, what he was and what he really wanted. He had adjusted to the challenge of being out in the real world, rather than in the monied goldfish bowl of privilege and low family expectations he had been raised in.

Below deck, Bunny settled into her bed, achingly tired but for that moment unable to sleep. She saw Sebastian's beautiful lean dark face afresh. Until him, she hadn't realised that a man could be beautiful or even that that single fact could be such a relentless draw for her. That was all that was the matter with her, she decided. It was just a stupid, physical thing. Nothing she need worry about. She didn't like him and that wasn't likely to change because he couldn't help himself and would probably screw up their next encounter. He had that rich, entitled vibe and she knew how a guy like that operated. Tristram had had the same vibe, same kind of fancy, aristocratic name, only she had been a very naïve teenager when she'd met him her first year of university. Shaking off those annoying memories, Bunny fell asleep.

When she wakened, she didn't at first realise why she was awake because it was still dark, only now the boat was rocking violently, and the wind was roaring. A storm, she registered in surprise, jumping out of bed fast and grabbing up her life jacket, throwing on her shoes and hurtling up topside to see if she could help.

A strange scene greeted her. The waves were terrifyingly high. Sebastian was nonetheless standing fully dressed like a statue while Reggie struggled frantically to tie down the mast. The mast had snapped and broken off low down, falling with sails still blowing madly. She was shocked, marvelling that such a thing could've happened, and she hastened over to Reggie, touching his back to let him know of her presence because the noise of the wind and the churned-up water made communication difficult. Why wasn't Sebastian helping? she wanted to ask and, since she couldn't, as Reggie whirled round she gestured at him and mouthed it.

Reggie yelled an answer but she didn't catch most of it, apart from, 'He's...stupid!'

He leant closer to her to make himself audible. 'Freak storm. Get him into the life raft with you. You've both got to get off *now*. She's heading for the reef and could capsize.'

'But what about you?' she shouted back in dismay.

'Staying with my boat. No arguments! Get on the

raft!' Reggie framed rawly, his urgency and attitude cutting through her anxieties, sending her straight into crisis mode.

The first day she had started work with Reggie he had taught her what to do in an emergency. She sped with care through every step exactly as he had shown her and all the while the catamaran was being pitched through the water like a child's toy. It was the most terrifying experience she had ever had and she could not understand why the only other able-bodied male on board was doing nothing. Or why Reggie was taking her very firmly by the elbow and ensuring that she got off the boat onto the raft safely, although she stumbled and lost one of her shoes in the water. She watched while Reggie sped back in the teeth of the wind to escort Sebastian as if he were a child needing guidance to join her. She supposed some people just froze in an emergency and he was one of them, seemingly quite impervious to the need to protect himself. Reggie thrust Sebastian down to collapse his legs. He had all the self-determination of a zombie.

Reggie tapped his head and looked at Sebastian. She wasn't sure quite what he meant but she nodded and then her skipper cut the line to release the raft and she was crawling under the canopy, so scared she didn't want to even see the rolling height of the waves sending the raft spinning across the water in a manner that put new meaning into the concept of being seasick. Her tummy heaved and she tried every calming method of breathing that she knew, fighting to keep a hold of her brain and not panic. When she finally glanced in Sebastian's direction again, she saw the rain washing away the blood on his neck and she crawled forward in even greater dismay, finally registering that he could be acting strangely because he had been injured before she'd joined him and Reggie on deck.

Guilt filled her because she had judged him for his silent inactivity, she *knew* she had. Dazed dark eyes gazed past her rather than at her. Was he concussed? Where was the blood coming from? Steadying herself on a lean powerful thigh, she used her other hand to reach up but he was too tall and it was too much of a stretch for her in a moving life raft that didn't feel steady or safe. She yanked off her life belt and tossed it over Sebastian's head, tying it, aware that just then he needed it more than she did. She gave up on the immediate need to locate his injury and caught his hand instead, yanking at it to try and get him under the canopy with her and out of the rain and wind. He was in some kind of daze, unable to do what was best for himself, which meant that that role fell on her. And she only had emergency first-aid training.

'Sebastian!' she shouted to him, as loud as she could, and yanked at his hand again with emphasis and, after a pronounced pause, he shifted his hips and edged painfully slowly under the shelter of the canopy with her.

And then just when she thought that she was getting somewhere with him, he slumped down flat as a pancake and closed his eyes. So, it didn't matter when she had to repeatedly throw up over the side of the raft when it went careening across the waves again as if it were a roller coaster. It didn't matter either when nature called because there was nobody to see once Sebastian had passed out.

Dawn was moving in and the sea was no longer so rough when Bunny managed finally to ease his head up and examine what she could with her fingers. A massive bump and swelling, she registered in horror. He was injured and Reggie had known it. Stupid, she had caught that one word, but he could have been saying 'half-stupid', which meant an entirely different thing. She smoothed his long black hair off his brow because his usual man bun had bitten the dust on deck at some stage.

She scrabbled for the emergency rations, tugging out the water with relief, not even caring about the brackish stale taste, only grateful that it was there. She shook Sebastian's shoulder but there was no rousing him. She rested a nervous hand on his chest, breathing again when she felt a strong, steady heartbeat. Somehow, she had to get water into him as well. She looked around. There was no land in sight, which was quite worrying when Indonesia rejoiced in almost eighteen thousand islands. Where were they anyway? Reggie had veered off his usual tried-and-trusted course, probably at Sebastian's behest, so when he came around, they would have a better idea of where they were, she thought hopefully.

The hours crawled past. She munched through a granola bar slowly and carefully. There were thirty days of rations on the raft. What had happened to Reggie? His wife would raise the alarm but not until the week's trip was officially past. Maybe he had managed to radio or call for help and survive. Her eyes stung. She was fond of Reggie, her father's old army mate. They would be found quickly, she assured herself, although the raft had been flung many miles from where *Merry Days* had lost her mast twelve hours earlier.

Sebastian stirred and instantly she was trying to get water into him. He grunted something and his eyes flew wide, finally focusing on her. He blinked. Still it seemed something of a blank slate.

'You need water,' she told him and his hand came up to grasp the bottle. 'You hit your head. You have concussion.'

He tried and failed to sit up and she guided the flow of water for him, not wanting any wasted. He wouldn't eat the granola bar she showed him. He was as stubborn as a pig, which wasn't a surprise. His eyes eased shut again but she chose to be cheered by the reality that he was more aware than he had been the night before. And then some hours later finally she saw what she had been waiting for, what she had expected much sooner: the sight of land. She dug out one of the little oars that was more for steering than passage in readiness and then they were coming in closer and, before the current could control them again, she was frantically paddling towards that distant beach.

She felt the raft catch below on the reef. There wasn't much choice, she thought. She hadn't planned to land over a coral reef with sharp points that tore at the raft in shallow water but getting onto dry land was the objective, especially with Sebastian comatose beside her. She yanked at the life belt to waken him and he half lifted, muttering something in some foreign language, belatedly reminding her that although he spoke perfect English, it was not his native tongue.

'Sebastian, we've got to get onto the beach!' she yelled, that having become her natural way of addressing him.

'Why are you shouting?' he asked.

Bunny grinned, delighted that he was that much closer to the real world inside his head. 'We have to get out of the raft onto the beach.'

Sebastian peered over the side and, presumably having estimated the depth, vaulted upright to immediately vacate the raft, which took her aback. For a split second she simply sat there disconcerted by that instant action before paddling more urgently towards the shore because Bunny was in survivalist mode and she wanted what remained of the raft as part of a shelter, reluctant to let it drift off before she had used it to the utmost. Her arms were ready to fall off by the time she beached the raft, aching like the very devil, and, by then, Sebastian had already stalked up the white-sand beach and headed for the shade provided by an outcrop of rocks. She clambered out into the water on the soft sand and thought, as she leant back to pull the raft up onto the shore, Yeah, he's every man for himself in an emergency, just what you would've expected, just what you would've feared.

In shock she watched as Sebastian began to undress, arranging his fancy sweater, a tee shirt and chinos over the rocks to dry in the sun. Nice to be wearing underwear, she reflected, stuck in her soaked pyjamas. But Sebastian sported boxers and even though they were perfectly respectable, she supposed, there was an enormous amount of Sebastian exposed. Her feet faltered in face of all that semi-nude male. The sheer expanse of bronzed, darkly shadowed torso, the big biceps, the map of eight-pack abs and the elusive vee of sheer muscle disappearing into the boxers, along with the long, powerful, hair-roughened thighs, were a traffic-stopping sight. Colour burned her face. If you didn't have boundaries, Sebastian was the guy to be stuck on a desert island with. And if she had the gumption, she would just be stripping off as well, ignoring the fact she'd be naked, simply concentrating on the fact that her clothing was wet.

Who the hell was she? Sebastian was wondering. Was she a girlfriend, or a stranger? She knew his name so she had to know him but *how* did she know him? After all, *he* didn't know him, didn't know what he had been doing on a life raft, didn't seem to know what day it was, never mind where he was and what he was doing. He lifted his hand to his long loose black hair and that didn't feel right either. When had he grown his hair so long? He traced the swelling at the back of his head and he knew he'd had medical training at that point because a stream of innate diagnoses was filtering into his thoughts. He had concussion, likely severe concussion, a post-traumatic brain injury including some degree of amnesia. Why else couldn't he recall what he had been doing *before* he got injured? And why wouldn't he just instantly come clean with his companion about what had happened to him? Why did he have an instinctive belief that he couldn't trust anybody?

'Why are you not wearing a life belt?' Sebastian asked as she drew close.

'I put mine on you…you weren't in any fit state to be without one. How's your head?'

Just his luck to be shipwrecked with a saint, he thought and then was dismayed by that cynical thought. She had done a kind thing, careless of her own safety, and why the hell would he be judging her for it? No, he wasn't himself, the self he had been the last time he had been in Indonesia, and yes, he was convinced that that was where he was. The smell of the air, the incredible coral reef below the clear water, the jungle landscape behind him. It was all achingly familiar but he also knew that he wasn't the lanky teenaged boy he had been on his last trip. No, he was a fully grown adult male with a big blank inside his head as if a wall had been built the year he reached twenty, shutting him out from his full self.

'Aching,' he admitted.

'You should rest,' Bunny told him anxiously. 'You were unconscious on the raft and you need to take care of yourself.'

'Of course,' Sebastian agreed, scrutinising her in minute detail. She was wearing what he reckoned had to be pyjamas because they had rainbow-coloured little ponies all over them. And she was almost unbearably cute, very small, dainty, bedraggled blonde hair loose nearly to her waist, luminescent green eyes, so frank and open against bare natural, freckled skin. 'But first, I intend to check out this place.'

Bunny stiffened. 'What do you mean?'

'Is this an island or a peninsula? We need to work out where we are—unless you know?'

'No, I don't,' Bunny admitted, taken aback to be faced with full-force Sebastian again, switched back on after being a zombie without self-determination. All that large personality and domineering nature confronting her? It was almost frightening and she took an actual step back from him. 'We were off course and the storm blew us for miles over a lot of hours.'

'Where were we last you knew?'

Bunny winced. 'Reggie didn't discuss the trip with

me. It wasn't his usual. As far as I'm aware it was in the direction *you* wanted to go and it was more remote,' she said uncomfortably.

'And Reggie?' Sebastian prompted.

'Reggie opted to stay with the catamaran, which he believed was about to drift onto the reef because the mast had snapped,' she explained dry-mouthed, wondering how many details he could recall, suspecting it would be few of the emergency that had landed them in unknown territory.

'So, you're crew and I was a passenger?'

'Not while we're *here*,' Bunny argued in a sudden urgent outburst. 'Here, wherever here is, we're *equals*!'

His ebony brows pleated. 'I wasn't aware that I was considering anything else. As I said, I'm off for a walk to explore this place.'

'Aren't you dizzy and weak?' Bunny pressed in growing astonishment.

'No, I'm not,' Sebastian lied without hesitation, spinning on his heel to walk down the beach past the rocks.

'What about your head?'

'A bruise and swelling. It'll be gone in a few days,' he said dismissively.

Bunny surveyed his bronzed back view with seething frustration. How was she supposed to let him walk off alone? Suppose he collapsed or fell? Wouldn't she be responsible for not taking better care of him? He wasn't sensible. How was that a surprise? And how was she supposed to control a man with such a dominant, forceful character? With a whip and a chair?

Snatching up a water bottle and a couple of the energy bars, she ran after him, drawing breathlessly level. 'Two heads are better than one.'

'Not in my experience,' Sebastian said smoothly, thinking of all the times during his education when stupid people had tried to misdirect his projects and derail him. He strode back down the beach to the raft and extracted the knife from the basic supplies. 'This should be useful.'

'Yes, I thought that we should stay on the beach and sort out some shelter for tonight.'

'We can still do that when we return.'

'But it could be dark by then!'

'I'll manage,' he assured her with complete confidence.

CHAPTER THREE

THEY FOLLOWED THE SHORE, sidestepping rocky outcrops in silence, and nowhere out to sea could she see any sign of other land but there was a misty haze in the distance and it could be blocking a clear view. Her legs got tired and keeping up with Sebastian was no easy task but she refused to ask him to slow down. She supposed he was right about the necessity of checking out their surroundings first.

'What year is it?' he shot at her abruptly.

Disconcerted, she told him, and he nodded, pausing to filch the water bottle from her and taking a swig, before passing it back to her and fluidly sinking down on the sand.

'Why did you ask me what year it was? Don't you know?'

'Head injury,' he reminded her calmly. 'Time is a bit confused for me right now. So...what's your name?'

'Bunny...no comments, please. You already made them once before.' But that fast she was also wondering why he didn't remember her name. 'Do you remember the catamaran? Reggie?'

'Not yet,' he admitted flatly. 'No doubt it'll all come back in good time.'

The last memory Sebastian had was of eating in a little bar at a harbour with his friends, who had drifted out to join him at different times that summer. Andreas had been there, his sister, Ariana, and a couple of others.

'Reggie's the skipper of the boat you hired on a private charter for a week. I'm afraid I don't even know how you got hurt. You were in a daze by the time I reached the deck in the storm,' she told him, handing him an energy bar.

Sebastian studied the bar and then accepted the inevitable: for now, it was all they had. He didn't think he had ever eaten anything that tasted like cardboard with grit before. Well, there was always a first time, but then survival on what he already suspected was a very small island would be a challenge even for him and he had cut his teeth on wilderness camping from an early age. Roughing it came surprisingly naturally to him. The horrors his relatives had heaped on him during his adolescence might actually turn out to be the key to survival. But what about her?

What about *Bunny*? Already skinny as a rail, wet clothes, legs trembling with a tiredness she struggled to hide, dark circles below her eyes. She had neither his strength nor, he believed, his high level of physical fitness on her side. Keeping Bunny breathing could be his biggest challenge. And she had given *him* her life belt! How could anyone be that selfless?

They rounded the cliff and then they were out on the far side of the island and Sebastian released a shout that startled her and started running down the beach. Bunny was so exhausted she wanted to fold where she stood but she kept on moving slowly in the same direction until she saw what had excited him. It was a little wooden pier poking out into the sea, an unlikely sign of human involvement in what seemed so far to be a small island wholly abandoned to the jungle and the birds. He disappeared from view, probably in the forlorn hope of finding a boat or a person, she guessed.

Sebastian was already surprising her on every level. He was very controlled and action orientated. He hadn't unleashed a single moan, the smallest hint of panic or even a word of complaint and yet, physically, he still had to be feeling pretty rough. Nor as a rich man could he be accustomed to moving out of his comfort zone. Their situation was hazardous and scary yet, if anything, danger appeared to fuel Sebastian's energy, lending a sharper edge to those shrewd dark eyes. And didn't he just look amazing clad only in a pair of cotton boxers, slung low on his lean hips? Her face burned and she scolded herself for noticing. He was as decent as he would've been in swimming trunks, which was, to be honest, *not* very decent.

Huffing a little from fatigue, she reached the pier and saw a small track leading through the dense overhanging trees. 'Sebastian!' she shouted, suddenly terrified of him vanishing and her being left alone.

'Over here!' he shouted back and then there was a deafening grinding, breaking noise that filled her with dismay and she pushed her woolly, heavy legs to move faster along the overgrown path until she arrived, shell-shocked, in a clearing that contained a house, a very fancy house on her terms, with the look of an architect-designed contemporary building and a deck furnished with an array of outdoor seating littered with branches and leaves.

'Right...' Sebastian appeared in front of her and dropped down to scoop her off her feet without the smallest warning. 'Now you can rest and stop quaking with terror.'

'I am not quaking with terror! What the heck are you doing?' Bunny gasped in disbelief as he carried her towards the house.

'Taking care of you,' Sebastian responded calmly, elbowing open a door and carrying her indoors, past an inner courtyard crammed with jungle plants and a strange indoor pool set in marble.

Without hesitation he settled her down on leopard-print velvet sectional seating in what had to be the most luxurious reception room she had ever seen. 'Wh-where's the owner?'

Sebastian squatted down in front of her, brilliant dark eyes level. 'How would I know? I broke in.'

'You...*what*?' she yelped in horror.

'This isn't a game, Bunny, this is survival. Here we will...hopefully...have water and shelter.'

Bunny gaped at him with frank incredulity. 'But you can't just break into someone else's house!'

'If it comes to a choice between living or dying I can.'

'Don't be stupid!' Bunny slung back at him in a temper. 'We'll be arrested and thrown in a cell!'

Sebastian chuckled. 'Someone has to rescue us first. I think I'll take that risk over being stuck here without shelter and the necessities of life. Now wait here until I can hopefully find you something to change into. Right now, in those wet pyjamas, you're asking for pneumonia and there's not enough flesh on your bones to stave it off.'

'We *can't* stay here, Sebastian,' Bunny moaned and with considerable personal regret on her own account. 'It's somebody's home.'

But Sebastian had already disappeared again. She blinked and literally felt herself zone out for a timeless period and it wasn't until Sebastian reappeared and tossed a man's shirt on her lap that she returned to the present.

'Can't stay here,' she mumbled afresh like a vinyl record stuck in a groove.

'Take off the damp clothing and put on the shirt,' Sebastian instructed impatiently. 'Because if you don't, I'm going to do it for you.'

'Like you would dare!'

'I would dare,' Sebastian assured her.

'Well, go away so as I can change.'

'Modesty in this situation is ridiculous,' Sebastian said very drily.

'Give me a break,' she muttered, and he strode over to the windows and slowly and rather ostentatiously turned his back on her. Unconcerned by that display, Bunny ripped off her pyjamas at speed and put on the plaid cotton shirt, shivering as she clumsily did up the buttons to cover her cold, clammy skin. Until that moment, she hadn't realised how cold she actually was.

'Now go for a sleep,' Sebastian told her.

'But—'

'You're dead on your feet and I don't want you getting sick.'

Bunny tugged a cushion under her head and curled up, too tired to deal with Sebastian, in truth too tired to deal with anything at all. The storm, the frightening sleepless night on the raft and the long hours that had followed were just a tangled jumble of shocking imagery inside her head. Something soft landed on top of her and she snaked her icy toes into the warmth it offered, her eyes sliding shut.

Sebastian was tired too, but he wanted to get the solar power on and the water running before he went to sleep and then had to waken in the dark. That achieved, he placed a lamp beside Bunny so that she wouldn't panic when she awoke and then he folded himself down on the opposite leg of the sectional.

The more he looked at her, the more beautiful she seemed to be. There was just something about her face, that particular arrangement of features, the delicate arch of her brows, the clarity of her big eyes, the smooth line of her nose and the natural pink of her lips, he reasoned absently, lost in a sense of fascination new to him. At least, it *felt* new.

Why was he so eager to look after her? Was there something crucial that he had forgotten? Had they been intimate on that boat? And what had he been doing on what sounded like a small boat in any case? It didn't make sense...none of it made sense and, on that edge of frustration, Sebastian finally slept.

Bunny opened her eyes and just lay there, listening to the incredibly noisy chatter of birds at dawn and, beyond that, the most glorious quiet, empty of other people's noises and traffic. Just about there she remembered that her student days were finished, and her eyes flew wide on an unfamiliar ceiling before lowering to take in the oil paintings of birds on the wall, the antique-looking bronze statues, carved mask faces and other paraphernalia displayed across a sleek, sealed glass display unit. It was someone's collection of Indonesian artefacts and a sobering reminder that she had spent the night in someone else's home without their permission. She was startled into sitting straight up and standing. There was no sign of Sebastian.

There was no reasonable explanation for why she

panicked when he was out of view. Maybe it was because being marooned on a rather small island with few, if any, edible resources was scary, but Sebastian seemed to have survivalist instincts that beat hers hands down. A more pressing need to find facilities, if there even were any indoors, gripped her and she went off to explore and found a door into a cloakroom behind that inside pond thing in the foyer. An ancient, battered man's jacket hung on the single peg. Not an owner with many visitors, she reckoned. In truth, a working facility with running water interested her much more just then. She studied the pond, empty of water, fish or greenery, and shrugged before heading down the corridor to find a staircase, which she climbed.

The whole time she was snooping, she was telling herself that Sebastian was right and they had to make the best of whatever fate had dealt them. There were only two doors, one of which led into a massive bedroom and en-suite bathroom. A door still hung open on a sparsely filled built-in closet, which Sebastian must've rifled through the night before to give her a shirt. The bathroom had a separate shower and bath, the appointments as opulent in finish as the huge four-poster steel bed, festooned with thin silky drapes to keep out insects at night. Giant windows overlooked the island interior and one set opened out onto a balcony with a single seat. The view over the palm trees and exotic jungle vegetation was magnificent and yet, even in the sunlight, it made her shiver and withdraw indoors again, painfully aware of their isolation and disconnection from the modern world.

Wouldn't the owner of such a fantastic house have an Internet connection and a computer? Heart hammering, she opened the second door into a home office with a desk but there was no tech in there of any kind and she left the room again with a grimace. Before she went downstairs again, she couldn't resist switching on the bathroom shower just to see if it worked and when it did, she was out of her borrowed shirt within seconds and stepping beneath that warm, rather than hot, flow. She didn't take her time. She washed and shampooed fast, unsure how much water she dared use. Emerging, she grabbed a towel and dried herself in guilty haste before donning the shirt, which was at least relatively clean even if she had slept in it.

She trod back down the stairs, embarrassed at having used the unknown owner's comb to untangle her long, knotty hair. When she walked through the last downstairs door, she found the kitchen: a gleaming state-of-the-art installation with stainless-steel utilities that looked as if it had never been used. A man's apron hung incongruously on another single peg. It was the cupboards that she was keenest to investigate in her search for food and just when she feared she'd drawn a blank she opened a large larder cupboard and found it packed with dry goods. Flour, coffee, sugar, salt, rice, pasta, quinoa and, below that, shelves of tins. Relief swept her in a wild rolling wave because with water, food and shelter they could manage for weeks, and surely it wouldn't *be* weeks before they were found?

Reggie would've called for help...but had he had time in the midst of that terrifying storm? And if he *hadn't* survived there would be no one alerted to their plight until his absence was noted. So, nothing certain, nothing sure as far as rescue went, she conceded reluctantly. Right now, they were stuck on this island in this house for the foreseeable future. The hungry growl in her stomach reminded her that she had more important things to concentrate on: food, because she was starving.

Sebastian returned from a busy morning on the beach, having gathered up his dry clothes from the rocks on his way, checked out the ripped remains of the life raft and set up a marker bonfire at the foot of the island. He walked back into the house and heaved a sigh, knowing that he had to eat. He was stunned into initial silence when he saw Bunny busily moving round the kitchen, covered in a giant navy apron.

'Who turned you into a Stepford wife?' he quipped.

Bunny froze and then spun round, a smile lighting up her face. 'Where have you been?' she demanded automatically. 'I mean, what is there to do out there? Where is there to go?'

Sebastian grinned with intense pleasure. 'Is this what being married feels like?'

A wash of pink swept over her expressive face and she turned away. 'I'm sorry, I—'

Amusement quelled, Sebastian rested his hands down on her narrow shoulders and turned her back from the sink where she was draining rice. 'It's okay. I was only teasing. You're very sensitive, aren't you?' he murmured, staring down at her with dark eyes lit by shades of caramel in the sunlit kitchen. 'Don't be that way with me. I'm…outspoken, loud, abrasive but I don't mean any actual harm.'

For an instant, Bunny was absolutely frozen where she stood, lost in the hold of those lustrous eyes of his and the kindness she saw there that he had not shown an ounce of on *Merry Days*. It made her feel all warm and soft inside, it made her want to stretch up and kiss him, a prompting that shook the life out of her and made her pull free and return to the rice.

'You're just in time to eat,' she muttered, shocked by the butterflies in her tummy, the clenching deep down inside. 'I'm afraid it's not cordon bleu exactly, it's tinned frankfurters and sauce and rice.'

'I'll go fishing for us.'

'That sweater needs washing,' she scolded. 'Although I doubt you'll ever get the bloodstains out of it.'

Sebastian laughed. 'Could I care less?' He tilted his head to one side, amusement glittering in his eyes and the curve of his mobile mouth. 'I don't think so but there is a washing machine in the utility area.'

'What utility area?'

As she was putting the food out, Sebastian crossed the kitchen to pull open the hidden door in the wall panelling. She finished setting the plates on the table and walked through. A complex array of levers, buttons and controls almost covered one entire wall and on the other sat a washing machine. 'So there's enough water here to use it freely?' she asked.

'Yes, it's a very expensive system, which I got working.'

'You did?'

'The power was off when we arrived and the water pump.'

Bunny nodded as she sat down at the table. 'So, you know how to work that kind of stuff?'

Sebastian shrugged rather than admit that he had been taken aback by how immediately he had grasped how everything worked, that he evidently knew and understood a lot about sustainable energy and, also, tech stuff. Last night he had dreamt of an algorithm that was somehow crucially important and his fingers had been flying over a keyboard. Piece by piece, who he was ten years on was emerging.

'I'd have been lost. I'm great with books, not so great at the practical stuff.'

He frowned. 'Books?'

'Yes, I'm starting my first job as a librarian when I get home... Gosh, it's only days away,' she voiced in consternation. 'Do you think they'll hold the job for me if I don't turn up?'

'You need to relax for now. I doubt if anyone even

knows we're missing yet,' Sebastian said and, although she had thought the same thing herself, it still cast her down to hear his confirmation of it.

'My family will be worrying. They're used to hearing from me every day.'

'*Every* day?' Sebastian said in wonderment at such family attention and affection as he lifted his knife and fork. 'You're British, aren't you?'

'Yes.'

'And you're this far from home and they're still expecting to hear from you *every* day?' he prompted. 'What age are you?'

'Twenty-three.' Bunny had flushed with embarrassment. 'We're just a very close family.'

Sebastian quirked an eloquent ebony brow. 'Did I sleep with you on that boat?' he asked without the smallest warning and with the utmost casualness.

Bunny almost choked on the food in her mouth. 'Er…no, that would be a definite no, Sebastian. In fact we didn't take to each other at all at first meeting.'

And then immediately he had to know all about that and she wished she had kept her tongue still in her mouth and said nothing, because she was forced to recount that story.

A faint flush highlighted his stunning cheekbones. 'I was rude to you…why?'

Bunny actually grimaced. 'Apparently you got the impression that I was attracted to you and you didn't like that.'

Sebastian nodded reflectively as he pushed the empty plate away, not enjoying what he was learning about his current self. Arrogant, rude, hurtful to a subordinate and all the things he had sworn never to be once he grew up.

'And was I right?' he prompted softly.

Bunny compressed her lips and tried to be the bigger, better person, who didn't lie. 'Yes, you were right, but nothing would have happened between us anyway because I'm not that kind of person.'

'And what kind of person is that?' he pressed. 'Considering that most of us have sex in our lives.'

'I wasn't being judgemental. I was just saying that I wouldn't sleep with someone only on the boat for a week's break!' Bunny fielded more sharply, her colour high, her exasperation with him extreme because he had no tact whatsoever. She rose and piled the plates and moved away from the table.

'Why?'

As she settled the plates into the sink, she was ready to scream. 'I'm not interested in one-night stands and I wouldn't embarrass Reggie, who is a good friend of my father's—'

'So, you wouldn't want word of your sex life travelling home? Is this Reggie that indiscreet?'

Bunny whirled round in a fury. 'Drop the subject, Sebastian, before I explode! We did not share anything on the boat but mutual antipathy, I assure you!'

'I appreciate that you find this discussion trying but I had to know how we interacted prior to coming here because I'm *very* attracted to you and I have to know where I stand with you.'

And with that, Sebastian sprang up with infuriating calm and walked out of the kitchen.

I'm very *attracted to you.*

Bunny was astonished. *That* hadn't occurred to her as a possibility on the boat or since. All of a sudden, he was forgiven for being so blunt and mortifying her. She understood now. That was why he had asked if they had had sex. He didn't remember the boat. But was being very attracted to her why he had been rude in the first place? No, that made no sense. He must've realised *after* he boarded. Bunny smiled. Well, fancy that!

Not that anything was likely to happen between them, of course. She and Sebastian were ships that passed and she didn't do casual. And wasn't that unfortunate? Bunny had only one man in her past and she had been in what she'd believed was a monogamous relationship with Tristram for most of the time they had been at university together. And then it had fallen apart once she'd discovered that he had been cheating on her all along. Even worse, she had learned that most of her friends and *all* of his had known that he was cheating. People didn't want to get involved these days but even though she understood that her friends had been afraid of telling her the truth, she still thought they could have hinted in any number of ways that Tristram led a double life. After all, her health could have been compromised by his infidelity.

Sebastian's sheer honesty was remarkably appealing to her at that moment as she relived that past. After what her family called the 'Tristram treachery', Bunny had been well warned not to get too involved with anyone she met fleetingly on her travels. And even though she was twenty-three and no longer an innocent, she had stuck to that rule to protect herself from further hurt. Not quite, though, how an adult woman should behave, she found herself thinking, dissatisfied with that fresh view of herself. Tristram had been a lying, cheating creep but she knew that not all men were the same.

She walked out of the kitchen and eventually walked round the whole house to establish that Sebastian had gone.

But he couldn't go far, she reminded herself as she made her way down to the beach. There was no sign of him and she set off along the shore, bare feet crunching on white sparkly sand in the sunlight. The island was divine from the lush green vegetation to the colourful birds and the empty beach of a dream holiday destination. But because she was stuck there against her will, it somehow felt like a prison. A prison with... *Sebastian*?

That was a whole other story, she conceded with a helpless grin. Few women would complain about being marooned with Sebastian. She would never have dared break into a stranger's house. He'd got them off the beach, he'd got the bathroom working and the power on. Even without his striking resemblance to a screen-star fantasy male, he would deserve an accolade for those accomplishments alone.

She was taken aback by the sight of Sebastian feeding a small bonfire at the bottom end of the island, near where they had arrived the day before. Only the *day* before, she reminded herself, and it was already shocking her that she felt so relaxed with him, as if he were a close friend, rather than a near stranger. Really, Bunny, she castigated herself, is this how you react to a very hot guy who admits that he finds you very attractive?

'So, this is what you've been at…you could've told me,' she remarked, striving not to be affected by the image of Sebastian in sunlight. He stood there so very tall and broad, luxuriant black hair tousled, dark eyes golden enticement in daylight and so handsome he made her teeth clench. 'I could've helped gather wood.'

'There are snakes in the undergrowth.'

And she couldn't help it, she shivered, not being a snake kind of girl. 'Why a bonfire? Hoping for passing shipping to notice?'

'I haven't seen a single boat since we arrived. No, the house obviously has a caretaker and presumably he's not that far away.'

'How do you know it has a caretaker and not just an owner?'

'There's no dust and nothing personal left in the

house aside from that collection of his and the paintings. The pool in the foyer has been emptied because, whoever he is, he's not been visiting much, but I believe the house is still being checked on at least a monthly basis,' he contended. 'If the caretaker sees smoke and we're even distantly in view of him, he will visit.'

'He might ask the police to visit.'

'Even better,' Sebastian contended with blazing confidence.

'I can't speak Indonesian beyond hello, goodbye and thanks,' she admitted.

'I speak enough to get by,' Sebastian said carelessly as she drew level. 'I spent a lot of time here sailing and exploring when I was a teenager.'

'With your parents?'

His lean strong features tightened. 'No, they… died years before.'

Embarrassed she had asked, Bunny nodded. 'That's tough.'

'Not really, particularly not when I see the level of supervision you're still receiving from yours,' Sebastian traded scathingly and then he stilled and frowned. 'My apologies, I shouldn't have said that.' In an abrupt volte-face, Sebastian bent down to grab up wood to feed the fire, his lithe, powerful length silhouetted against black swirling smoke.

But he had been deflecting sooner than address the topic of parents, Bunny recognised, wondering why that was such a sore spot apart from the obvious reason of loss, particularly when that loss had taken place years back in his distant past. At most, she reckoned he was in his very early thirties, and it was a little odd to still be *that* sensitive. Only what did she know about such emotions when she had yet to lose anyone she loved?

Surely, she *had* to know about his parents, Sebastian was thinking. Everyone knew that horror story! He was the survivor of his family, a victim, which he hated to acknowledge especially when the relatives treated him as though he were mentally unstable and somehow fatally contaminated like his late father. Arrogant much, Pagonis? Of course, not every chance-met stranger knew his history but, with his inherited wealth, people were usually quick to look him up online and then they found out because it was all still out there for anyone to see.

'How much do you know about me?' Sebastian shot at her without warning.

'Nothing, well…three facts. I know your first name and that you were born in Greece and that there's a rumour that you're very rich,' she told him uneasily.

'Didn't you look me up online?'

'Not on my phone budget on a boat abroad,' Bunny admitted. 'I usually use the bar at the harbour for Internet access and send messages or call home while I'm there. I've lived on the boat since I arrived. What's your surname? Would I know it?'

'A lot of people do… Pagonis.'

'Sorry, not familiar at all. Pagonis...' she sounded out absently.

Sebastian was amused, oddly relieved by her ignorance of his background. For once, it seemed, he was on a level playing field with a woman. 'And yours?'

'Woods...'

Sebastian flung back his handsome head and laughed with appreciation. 'Bunny Woods. Nobody was thinking too hard when they named you, but you are undeniably cute.'

Bunny went pink and collided with smouldering dark golden eyes that burned through her like a shot of adrenalin. She rushed into speech. 'I was thinking that we could make a big SOS message on the beach with stones or shells or something...seaweed?' she asked uncertainly. 'In case a plane flies over. I know we haven't heard any yet, but we should be prepared just in case.'

'That's a good idea,' Sebastian commented, walking over to her, lean hands lifting to rest lightly on her slight shoulders. 'Are you going to feel threatened if I kiss you?'

'Will *you*? No telling what a sexually deprived woman might do to a man without backup on a remote island,' she teased.

'No telling.' Enjoyment gleamed in Sebastian's heavily lashed eyes, whirls of caramel and whiskey shades in the darkness of those eyes that made her heart beat so fast, it felt as if it were sitting right at the back of her throat. Her bare feet felt welded to the sand as though she couldn't have moved even if she had wanted to. She was feeling an excitement absolutely new to her that she had not known even in the heady first days with Tristram, and that sense of thrilling anticipation was uniquely seductive. Of course, deep down inside, she expected to be vaguely disappointed as usual.

Sebastian gazed down into her intent green eyes, a sort of witchy green, he decided. He remembered hanging an old green glass fishing buoy in a window as a kid, daydreaming that it was a magic witch's ball that he could somehow escape his life through. He didn't know what it was about Bunny, but she soothed him in some weird way, made him want to be a better man than he believed he was. The way he had spoken to her when he boarded that boat? As if she were nothing, nobody. He didn't want to be that man but, apparently, he *was* that man ten years at least down the road.

He ran slow fingers across her delicate collarbone, tracing it, following the line of her slender neck, cupping her pointed chin, and then let go, bending to lift her gently off her feet and rest her down horizontally on the sand. 'No way of doing this comfortably when we're standing. You are way too small and I am way too tall,' he sighed, folding down and holding his weight off her with one powerful arm.

'You about to whip out a tape measure or kiss me?'

'I didn't want to scare you.'

'I get that...but *still* waiting here,' she countered with a lively smile of one-upmanship.

And then he just kissed her, kissed her long and deep and slow and every nerve ending in her body came alive as though it was a celebration rather than an experiment on her part. Never had she felt like that before. Never had anything felt so intense that her entire body felt engaged in a cliff-edge scream for more. The delve of his tongue made her spine arch and jackknifed her up into closer contact. And he came down on top of her in a wildly hungry kiss that sent every nerve ending in her body pulsing and begging. Her nipples tightened into hard buds as his chest shifted over hers and a throbbing helpless heat pooled between her thighs. And it was too soon, way too soon for that and way too *dangerous*, her brain shouted at her, dragging her free of the erotic spell he cast. She liked to think through such actions, to look and ponder before she leapt. Sebastian intoxicated her and on some level that was as scary as it was exhilarating.

Opting out, Bunny tried to shift sideways, which was impossible beneath his weight, but he got the message and folded back onto his knees. 'For one kiss, that was amazing.'

'Who are you trying to kid? That was at least ninety-five kisses. Take your clothes off,' she told him, eying the blood stain on that gorgeous sweater.

For a split second, Sebastian froze and then vaulted upright as Bunny got up as well. He peeled off the sweater and the tee shirt, embarked on his salt-stained chinos, only to freeze as she yelped, 'No, not the boxers too!'

No, not a shy bone in this guy's body, she thought with roaring appreciation as she gathered up the sweater, tee shirt and chinos and turned on her heel to head smartly back to the house.

'Where are you going?'

Bunny flipped him a glance over her shoulder and laughed. 'I'm planning to try out the washing machine...'

She swore that she would cherish the incredulous look on Sebastian's darkly handsome face until her dying day.

CHAPTER FOUR

'YOU'RE CLEVER,' SEBASTIAN commented over an evening meal of freshly grilled fish, which he had supplied, and freshly made bread, which she had baked.

'How?' she challenged although she knew perfectly well, for that afternoon had passed with both of them laying out an SOS message on the beach on both sides of the island. Palm leaves weighted down with stones had worked the best. And Sebastian had been kind of quiet and broody.

'When you told me to undress, you *knew* what—'

'Of course, I did,' she said lightly. 'But it's not that simple, Sebastian. I'm not ready to take that step with you.'

His wide sensual lips compressed hard. 'That's fine.'

'And maybe you haven't thought of it, but I have... Have you any contraception?'

His ebony brows lifted and dropped again, his lustrous dark eyes steady while his lush black lashes dipped. 'As a matter of fact, no. But surely *you*—?'

'What I was using was left behind on the catamaran.'

In the simmering silence, Sebastian breathed in deep and smiled at her, a level smile that surprised her. 'I should've thought of that aspect. I'm afraid I didn't.'

'And I'm afraid I'm naturally sensible and cautious,' Bunny confirmed quietly.

'As a rule, I am too,' he told her, his brilliant dark eyes narrowing. 'But, *not* with you for some reason. Don't look so anxious. But I will certainly cherish that moment when you told me to take my clothes off for many years...and then took them away to wash them.'

'I didn't want to argue with you. I didn't want a confrontation.'

'Listen...' Sebastian closed a hand over hers with complete casualness and smiled at her. 'A woman doesn't ever have to apologise for being clever when she's saying no. I'm not the type of guy who will ever quarrel with that but, be warned, I *am* the kind of man who will think of all the *other* things we can do.'

'Understood,' she said a little breathlessly, her colour high.

'You've been bitten,' he pointed out, indicating the swelling on her arm.

'Last night,' she said with a shrug.

'You won't be bitten tonight. We're both sleeping with the insect drapes around us upstairs.'

Bunny bit at her lower lip.

'And you will be perfectly safe in that bed with me,' Sebastian assured her smoothly.

Bunny didn't think she would be safe even in an Arctic environment with Sebastian, never mind a big, comfy bed. Furthermore, her pyjamas weren't dry as yet, which meant sleeping in the shirt again. She breathed in deep and asked herself if she was really that concerned. And she wasn't. She trusted Sebastian, didn't know why but she simply did. In her opinion he was too outspoken to be a habitual liar.

'How long do you think it will take for us to be found?'

'It could be a couple of weeks until a search finds us and I doubt if we're even officially missing yet. We'll conserve the tinned and dried goods and I'll fish,' Sebastian informed her.

Bunny tried not to think of the horror that would assail her family when or if they were informed that she had gone missing at sea. In an effort to move on from that thought, she said, 'Who do you think owns this place?'

'A keen birdwatcher with enough cash to build his dream hideaway in the back of beyond,' Sebastian opined with a frown. 'Someone older than us, I suspect, and there's no sign of a woman or guests ever having been here. I'll compensate the owner for everything we've used, broken or ruined.'

'I suppose that's all you can do,' Bunny muttered, thinking that there really wasn't anything else to eat on the island unless they started trapping birds and she recalled Reggie telling one of their hunting-mad passengers that it was forbidden on most of the islands they visited.

She tried to get into a book on birds and soon found herself yawning. Sebastian had taken himself off again. He was like that: restless, always needing an occupation or a challenge. She went upstairs and had a brief shower, put a replacement head on the electric toothbrush and freshened up. Pleasantly sleepy, she unfurled the drapes right round the bed and crept in one side. She wondered if she should put a pillow down the middle of the mattress and grimaced at an idea that would only make Sebastian laugh at her.

A while later, she was vaguely aware of Sebastian's return, the sounds of him undressing, the beat of the water in the fabulous shower and she turned towards him as the mattress gave beneath his weight.

'Go back to sleep,' he whispered.

'My mind is too busy. I was thinking of the last time I shared a bed on a regular basis... Not a happy place to revisit,' she muttered ruefully and ready to kick herself.

Sleepy Bunny was confiding Bunny, Sebastian registered, and he grinned. 'Something bad happen?'

'My ex had been cheating on me from the start and I was with him for over two years before I found out. How sad is that?'

'Are *you* still sad about it?'

'Heavens, no! It's way over a year since we broke up. I'm only sad that I didn't catch on sooner. I wasted a lot of time at uni with him when I could've been out having fun.'

'Learn from it,' Sebastian advised, sliding an arm round her and easing her closer. 'Don't get all your hopes and dreams tangled up with one person. It doesn't work. People almost always let you down.'

And where did that depressing belief come from? Sebastian questioned inwardly, positively chilled by what he had said. People could be fast friends and dependable. Yes. He had collided with a lot of the other sort in life but the few close friends he had he trusted completely.

'Kiss me goodnight,' he said abruptly.

'It won't stop at one kiss.'

Sebastian laughed with rich appreciation. 'Is that me or you you're condemning?'

'Both of us,' she traded, her cheek resting against his shoulder, her body relaxing into the heat and the already familiar scent of him. 'Let's be sensible.'

'I don't think I've ever heard a gloomier piece of advice from a woman.'

'You're more daring than me.'

'Daring is more fun,' Sebastian chided, rolling over and gazing down at her in the moonlight, his tousled dark head descending slowly.

And she knew he was giving her time to pull away if she chose but her brain was preoccupied with wondering if she had had *any* fun since childhood. She didn't think so, aside from the very occasional night out with friends. She had toed the line Tristram had laid out like that Stepford wife that Sebastian had mentioned, and the memory stung. Her ex hadn't liked her going out with friends but most likely, she acknowledged now, that had been because he was afraid of her seeing him out cheating on her. It struck her that she had spent most of her life doing what other people believed she should do, first her family and then her ex.

Irritated by that thought that she had never yet claimed the freedom to be herself, she tipped her head back and trailed her soft full lips over Sebastian's and he took the hint like a trooper. She was a little better prepared for that sensual onslaught than she had been earlier in the day.

Even so, that unfamiliar jolt of pure excitement still shook her up. He was one hell of a kisser. Fingers sliding through her hair, he flattened her to the bed and kissed her breathless. She was conscious of every hard, sculpted angle of his big, powerful physique. A little shiver feathered through her in response to the hard masculine arousal pressed against her. And then before she could even catch her breath, Sebastian was pulling back and settling her back on her own side of the bed.

'Night, Bunny.'

'Night,' Bunny whispered shakily, knowing she wished he hadn't stopped, knowing she had been burning up to touch him and feel him touch her, but clearly the fun had gone out of it for him. Served her right too for holding so fast to her boundaries. She wasn't a teenager any more or a born-again virgin. Tristram had taught her a hard lesson but he hadn't broken her, hadn't reduced her to a timid woman, afraid of her own shadow or her desires.

Why wasn't she being honest with herself? She wanted Sebastian more than she had ever wanted any man and she might never get another chance to explore that side of herself with such a perfect partner. Sebastian was experienced, sophisticated, gorgeous... Tick, tick, tick, he checked every box. In addition, she was never going to see him again once they got off the island and wasn't that even more perfect? Sebastian as a wicked one-off experience? Wasn't that much safer than attaching all sorts of foolish emotions to how he could make her feel? And then another rather frightening thought occurred to her and she burst into speech.

'You're not married or engaged or anything...are you?'

Sebastian froze. 'Absolutely not. I'd be wearing a wedding ring if I was married and I've never seen the point in engagements.'

And all of that was true...totally, sincerely true.

'I didn't think so but I found myself needing to check,' Bunny muttered and, before she could lose her nerve, she slid under the sheet that covered them, small smooth hands travelling across his torso and down a long, powerful, hair-roughened thigh.

And Sebastian jerked rigid with shock, total, complete shock as his somewhat proper, blushing companion set about boldly pleasuring him. Just as quickly he relaxed back in the moonlight, enchanted by her sheer unpredictability and the discovery that she could make him crave her caresses like a narcotic. She wasn't skilled or practised but she made up for that with enthusiasm. It wasn't very long before Sebastian was pushing the sheet back, tossing it back out of reach when she tried to hide below it again and long brown fingers settled into the silky depths of her hair to encourage her as his hips rose. He pulled away from her to climax with a guttural groan and flopped back against the pillows.

'That was unbelievably good. I suspect we're both stressed as hell in this situation,' Sebastian sighed as he tugged her back to him. 'And now it's my turn.'

'Nobody needs to take turns!' Bunny gasped, already embarrassed by the intimacy of what she had chosen to do.

'I'm eager to touch you, so no invitation is required,' Sebastian groaned, leaning down to kiss her with languid expertise, his tongue darting, his fingers releasing the buttons on the shirt she wore one by one.

Bunny dragged in a stark breath, insanely conscious of the tightness of her nipples and the heavy ache at the heart of her. He spread the shirt open, kissed her again, slowly, savouring her response. And she thought, This is not me, I am not a fun girl, I'm serious and I don't fool around.

But is that set in stone? another voice demanded.

Or can you go off the rails now and again? She was going off the rails but what did it say about her that she didn't *care* just at that moment?

His big hands covered her breasts, teased at her nipples and a slight sound escaped her lips as he shifted position, moving over her, bringing his mouth down to her breasts, toying with the tender tight peaks until she squirmed, hot liquid heat pooling in her pelvis.

'May I put the light on? I want to see you.'

Her teeth clenched on a negative. She was accustomed to the privacy of the dark but with Sebastian, she reckoned, she should've known better. 'If you like...'

He leant over her and lamplight momentarily blinded her. Sebastian gazed down at her anxious face, stunning black-lashed dark eyes intent on her. 'Stop freaking out.'

'I'm not freaking out!'

'It's in your eyes, *kounelaki mou*,' he commented. 'Yet you didn't freak out on the life raft or during the storm, did you?'

'I was freaking out inside myself.'

'But you handled it, so why can't you handle me doing a perfectly normal thing like admiring these very pretty breasts?' he asked softly, one big hand cupping her pert, swollen flesh while his thumb rubbed at the straining pink tip.

And she shivered with reaction, entrapped by his spellbinding gaze until he dropped his head and laved that prominent peak with his tongue before tugging at it with his lips. She closed her eyes and relaxed a tiny amount because he was moving slowly, gently. She tensed when his hand travelled over her stomach and roamed further south, probing the soft damp curls on her mons, teasing her slender thighs apart and then she literally jerked when he stroked her where she so ached to be touched, and her face burned. The first hints of pleasure were almost all-consuming, her hips lifting and tiny noises escaping her as he teased her sensitive entrance.

'You're so wet, so tight,' he husked, shimmying down her body and disconcerting her more than a little by settling himself between her thighs.

'Oh, you don't need to do *that*,' she muttered in mortification because her one and only lover had cringed at the very prospect.

'I want to. I very much want you to enjoy being with me.'

'Oh?' She had nothing to say to that, hadn't really believed that some men thought like that, and she didn't want him to stop what he was doing. Indeed, just then she was on the edge of anticipation as he explored her where she tingled and *needed*. The pulse of hunger climbed ever higher.

And just there the dialogue died because rather suddenly she couldn't have vocalised a word. Sebastian devoured her like a man at a banquet who hadn't eaten in days and she was shocked by that hungry passion for *her* body while she was overwhelmed by sensation. The pleasure built and built like a knot tightening ever more inside her until all she could do was yield to it as he drove her to a peak and she cried out loud as explosive pleasure gripped her, her fingers lost in the luxuriant depths of his hair as her spine arched and blissful waves of delight convulsed her. The fact that she had reached a climax, that there had been no need to fake it, shook her the most.

'Wow,' she mumbled in a wobbly voice. 'You're pretty good at that.'

'I'm a perfectionist. If I promise to pull out, may I continue?' Sebastian asked, convinced that there would not be that great a chance of an unwanted pregnancy engulfing them.

Bunny stiffened. 'But…that's not foolproof.'

'No precautions are foolproof.'

Long brown fingers framed her chin as she lowered her lashes. 'What you really need to know is that if there *are* consequences, I'll be there for you.'

'Doubtful,' she dared to remark. 'When we leave the island, we'll both go back to our own lives.'

'That doesn't mean I'll behave like a bastard or mistreat you. Whatever happens, you can depend on me.' Brilliant dark eyes held hers fast. 'I will support you. I promise you that. I'm not the least bit irresponsible.'

And that she *did* believe. Impatience and frustration engulfed her as she hesitated and then the reckless impulse that had landed her deep into Sebastian's arms took over again. She was going to bury any last memory of Tristram and the damage he had inflicted so deep that she would never think about him again.

'Yes,' she whispered shakily, proud of herself for wanting to move forward and open herself to new experiences with someone else.

'I'll make it good,' he swore.

He stroked her sensitive nub again, refreshing the desire that had gone into temporary abeyance. Her body jolted back to life, hunger and desire stirring afresh. She linked her arms round his neck, no longer worried about the light, indeed revelling in the glory of Sebastian over her with his long black hair tossed by her fingers, his jawline dark with stubble, his lean, dark perfect features taut with craving for her. Without warning she felt like the hottest woman on planet Earth. *He* made her feel like that where Tristram had left her feeling inadequate and manipulated, stupid and trusting.

Sebastian rearranged her lower limbs like an artist and shifted over her before hoisting her legs over his shoulders. 'The look of dismay on your face is precious,' Sebastian quipped. 'But I'm not going to hurt you.'

'I know that!' she gasped, eyes burning with the threat of tears because he had read her face and she would sooner he had not.

'If you want to stop, tell me at any stage.'

'Stop fussing,' she urged, her cheeks burning.

He pushed into her slowly and she shut her eyes again, enthralled by that stretching invasion of her channel, and then he sank deep and a little whimper was wrenched from her. It felt so good she was struggling for breath, struggling to stay silent. She had never been a screamer but she suspected that Sebastian had the power to turn her into one. The sensations gathered and pulsed at her core and she melted like honey heated under a grill, the throb of desire a relentless pull on every sense. The scent of his skin, the smooth bronzed satin of his shoulders and back, the raw intensity of his glittering black diamond eyes all held her fast.

He shifted pace, driving into her, sliding out, returning again with a sensual twist of his lithe hips that sent excitement flaming through her. And the erotic thrills only increased when he speeded up, pausing to stroke her again and ensure that she was pitched as high as he was. It was like nothing she had ever experienced, and yet it was everything she had ever dreamt of finding in intimacy.

She opened her eyes to enjoy him again and he stole a deep, driving kiss, his tongue delving in erotic mimicry of his possession. In that moment she felt as though he owned her very soul. A visceral hunger spread as he pushed her to ever greater heights. Her heart was thundering, her whole body given over to the pleasure and she surrendered her control to it, holding back nothing as the burning excitement enveloped her and splintered through her in a wondrous explosion of searing pleasure. She was only dimly aware of Sebastian hitting the same high with a masculine growl and the dampness as he spilled on her stomach and she flopped back boneless on the bed, totally wrecked.

Sebastian slid out of bed, stalked into the bathroom and returned some minutes later to wipe her clean. 'Now you can go to sleep without fear of the big bad wolf pouncing.'

'I quite like you pouncing,' she mumbled round an uncontrollable yawn.

'I like you pouncing on me even better,' he countered and that was the last thing she remembered for some time.

Sebastian watched her burrow under his arm and throw a leg over his. He didn't think he liked that kind of togetherness because he could feel some inner part of him recoil but, for some reason, he rather liked it with her. He felt oddly guilty though, rather as though he had seduced her. He was pretty sure that she wasn't very experienced and that he was *her* walk on the wild side. Nothing wrong with that, was there? Was it because she made him feel oddly protective? But how the hell could he protect her from himself?

He knew the effect that he could have on the wrong kind of woman. He knew that for a reason he would never forget. Years had passed but the trauma of dealing with Ariana had marked him deep, taught him to be careful around certain women. But much more important questions beyond the temporary amnesia afflicting him were gradually driving him crazy. Who was he *now*? Ten years on, ten years more mature? Had he graduated as a doctor? Had he gone on to train as a surgeon? Or somewhere along the road had he fallen by the wayside, distracted by some other discipline, some other interest? Why did he yearn for a keyboard? Why did he dream of strings of coding and did that excite him more?

And was his grandmother, Loukia, even still alive well into her eighties? His stomach churned at the fact that she might not be because she was the only relative he had ever cared about or fully understood. He knew exactly why Loukia had chosen not to raise her orphaned grandson, of course he did. She had raised his father, Jason Pagonis, and that had gone badly wrong for all of them. She had been afraid of it happening again with Sebastian and had stepped back, ultimately failing him by sentencing him to the care of those who despised and resented him because of the blood in his veins and his inheritance. The blood of the eldest and once favourite son, Loukia's heir.

Bunny wakened in an empty bed and headed for the shower straight away. Predictably her thoughts had gone straight to Sebastian, but she didn't censure herself for that truth because she knew that her best chance of surviving being stranded meant relying on him.

After all, she would have let herself almost starve and die before she broke into someone else's house and by then she might've been too weak to do it. If she had thought of a bonfire, she probably would have run at the first sign of a snake or, worse, got bitten. She could've fished but not at the rate Sebastian was fishing, so she wasn't at all surprised to go downstairs and find fish already deboned and ready for cooking. He was very efficient, but he wasn't telling her the whole story about his current condition.

'I'd be wearing a wedding ring if I was married.'

A telling choice of words. Did that mean that Sebastian didn't actually know for sure? Or that he was relying on his lack of a ring to convince him? Did Sebastian not actually remember such facts yet? She recalled him asking what year it was and winced. Exactly how extensive was his memory loss? And wasn't it time she found out?

She had two pairs of old, worn jeans on the table when Sebastian reappeared, bringing with him the scent of fresh smoke. He wore only his boxers and she believed that those were for her benefit because she suspected that without her presence, Sebastian wouldn't be wearing any clothes at all. He was perfectly at home in his own skin and he looked amazing, aglow with bronzed vitality, a walking, lean, powerful temptation of a male with wide shoulders, a heavily muscled torso, lean hips and long, strong legs. In spite of her best intentions, heat surged between her thighs like a betrayal. His stunning dark eyes gleamed like melted caramel in sunshine.

'What are you doing?' he asked, indicating the jeans she had spread out.

'We need clothes. I thought I could cut these jeans down into shorts so that we had a change, at least,' she said tautly. 'Could we talk before I grill breakfast?'

His lean, strong features tensed and shadowed. 'You've had second thoughts about us last night,' he assumed.

'Yes and no,' she responded awkwardly, unwilling to get into that difficult conversation without having got her thoughts together. 'But it was your memory loss I was keen to ask more about. How much have you forgotten?'

'The past ten years. The last thing I now actively recall I was heading towards my twentieth birthday and on a sailing holiday here,' he admitted flatly. 'I was a medical student then.'

'Oh, my goodness, I slept with someone who was mentally a teenager last night!' Bunny gasped, taken aback by the amount of time he had lost to amnesia and how carefully he had kept that information to himself. He might be outspoken but that didn't mean he would ever be a mine of freely offered information, especially not if he deemed it *personal* information, she acknowledged.

'I suspect I must've been unconsciously drawing on knowledge I didn't have at nineteen,' Sebastian informed her drily of the night before.

Bunny felt hot colour sweep her from throat to brow and looked at the fish instead.

'A lot of knowledge is still in my head if something jogs my memory,' he confided. 'My dreams are full of flashes of imagery that are unfamiliar to me in the present, a sign, I would imagine, that my memory will soon right itself.'

'And yet you confidently told me that you were single!' Bunny condemned anxiously, switching on the grill, fumbling with the fish to keep her hands busy.

'I am confident of that. I'm a loner. I don't believe in for-ever-and-ever vows. In fact, you could say I was biased against marriage. I don't believe I could've changed *that* much.'

'A lot changes in ten years. Ten years ago, I was breaking my heart for a weirdly dressed guy in a boyband!'

Sebastian shrugged. 'I was never the idolising sort. I was a nerd. I had sex but I didn't date or have relationships.'

'You sound emotionally repressed,' Bunny remarked. With determination, she moved to hold a pair of jeans up against his long legs and mark them with the pen she had found, so that she would know where to use the scissors. 'Crushes are a healthy step on the way to adult relationships.'

As she straightened up again, the ache between her legs intensified, a reminder of the intimacy *she* had instigated. She had yet to get past that shocking fact, that *she* had practically invited him to have sex with her. Reckless! Or *had* it been reckless? Hadn't it been more a case of her stepping into her future of freedom, unrestrained by other people's boundaries? Her decision for once rather than someone else's choices and beliefs limiting her.

Yesterday's bread was stale, and she had toasted it because Sebastian had put an embargo on using the flour in an effort to slow down their use of the ready food in the larder. She set condiments on the table and made coffee. Black for both of them, sugar in only hers and the sugar was running low. Soon, she would have to go cold turkey, but for all her protests she really wasn't sure that she could go cold turkey on Sebastian, who lit up the room with his energy simply by entering it. His charisma was as unnervingly strong as her own fascination.

'Do you have five minutes free so that I can shout at you?' Sebastian enquired quietly.

'Why would you want to shout at me?'

Sebastian dealt her a grim appraisal. 'Because I found the distress flares unused in the life raft...why the hell didn't you send them up during the storm?'

CHAPTER FIVE

Bunny's smooth brow furrowed and then eased again. Sebastian was studying her with frowning annoyance and her tummy turned over sickly. She decided to be honest. 'I forgot about them.'

'You...*forgot*?' he shot back at her in disbelief, studying her intently. Could anyone possibly be that honest?

Sebastian had little experience of such open behaviour. He was accustomed to lies and half-truths at best. Her candour had blown his anger back on him. He was in a volatile mood and thoroughly unsettled because his memory was returning in snatches. He had recalled being on a surgical rotation at a hospital, so he must have completed his medical degree if he had still been training. But he had also recalled burning the candle at both ends while he struggled to solve a tech security problem. Clearly, his once wholehearted approach to medicine had faltered at some point.

Bunny nodded vigorously. 'In the storm, the raft was pitching about and I was trying to keep my balance and watch yours as well. I was also throwing up a lot and terrified. Reggie never mentioned the flares or told me how to use them.'

'It's simple. You point and fire,' Sebastian incised curtly, exasperated that they might just have missed their chance of an immediate rescue. 'There may have been people on land or shipping nearby.'

'But there just as easily might not have been,' she pointed out in her own defence as she set out the food. 'This island was the first land I saw. Reggie only trained me on how to launch the raft. He never showed me the equipment on it.'

His ebony brows lowered. 'That is as may be but common sense should've urged you to—'

'Well, it didn't, no point crying over what's already behind us,' Bunny said in a deliberately upbeat tone, determined not to have her oversight become the focus for a useless argument. 'Now you've got them to use here at the right moment.'

Sebastian glowered at her. 'I *think*—'

'No, I don't want to hear any more about it,' Bunny told him with brisk finality. 'I plead guilty to a mistake. Now sit down and eat your breakfast.'

Sebastian compressed his wide mobile lips like a grump, but he settled down at the table to lift his coffee. 'You don't like confrontation. That doesn't work with me.'

'We're both trying the best we can to get through this. Let's not make mountains out of molehills.'

His eyes glittered like black ice. 'The homely cliché only sets my teeth on edge.'

'Sorry.' She was disconcerted by that sudden chill in the air and she addressed her attention to her plate. She would've liked to have screamed at him about that horrendous, terrifying night on the raft during the storm, when she might as well have been alone. So, she hadn't been perfect but she had kept them both safe long enough to reach land. 'But you have to accept that I'm not a seawoman or whatever you call it. Reggie gave me my first job on a boat and my *only* experience of sailing and it would take torture and intimidation to get me on *any* kind of a boat again!'

He sprang upright and cleared the table. 'I love being on the water. It relaxes me.'

Bunny said nothing, although she was tempted to remind him that he had been protected from the ordeal by his comatose condition. She wiped down the table before laying down the jeans to cut them.

Sebastian startled her with an intervention because he didn't like the atmosphere he had created. He didn't like arguing or even *trying* to argue with her. He didn't like the distance that was threatening to stretch between them and, in reaction, he curved his hands to her hips and carried her into the opulent reception room, dropping down on the sectional with her splayed across his thighs.

'What are you doing? I was about to cut those jeans down.'

'They'll take a rain check... I'm not as forgiving,'

Sebastian contended. 'Let's wind back a few minutes. If you'd still been in bed when I returned, I'd have climbed back into bed with you. If you'd been a little more receptive, I'd have stripped you in the kitchen.'

'Sebastian,' she argued, mortified because she could fully imagine either scenario. Unlike her, he was very upfront in his attitude to sex.

Without warning, his passionate mouth crushed hers with hungry urgency and her lips parted, instinctively allowing him access. He lifted his head again, dark eyes fiercely intent on her face. 'You want to stop this? Say so now.'

Small fingers reached up to his stubbled jawline and smoothed, her luminous green eyes wide and troubled because she didn't want to wind him up. She wanted him to calm down, although she was still wounded by his criticism of her actions during the storm. 'I don't know what I want yet. We were in that bed before I registered that anything had started.'

In answer to that response, Sebastian swung her off him to set her down with care beside him. 'It's your choice. I'm on fire for you but if you would prefer to call a halt, I won't put pressure on you to change your mind.'

'I've only ever been in one relationship,' she admitted unevenly, embarrassed to admit that lack of experience. 'And you say you don't do relationships at all. I'm not like that. But I do know that what we've got is just for now and is probably only happening because we're stuck here alone together.'

'We don't need to have this discussion. But please don't start imagining that you're falling in love with me.'

Her eyes flew wide. 'Why would you say *that* to me? Am I acting like that?'

'No.' Sebastian vented his breath in an impatient hiss and then sighed heavily, thinking back to his unfortunate experience with Ariana. 'But once a girl I looked on like a sister decided she was in love with me and became obsessive about it.'

Immediately, Bunny was listening. 'Who was she?'

'Ariana, the kid sister of one of my best friends. She travelled here with her brother and me. I was eighteen. She was a year younger. There was nothing between us and never had been. Her brother thought it was funny…just a silly infatuation, but he insisted that I had to be frank with her and tell her that I wasn't interested. I did and she took an overdose and almost died.'

Bunny flinched, clear green eyes flying to his in dismay and sympathy. 'Oh, no…'

'When Ariana recovered, she was depressed and her family put her in a clinical support unit because they were afraid she would try again. I felt responsible even though I hadn't encouraged her. I may not remember the last few years but I'm always careful to set that one rule if I see the same woman more than once. If you should ever feel that you can't live without me, walk away fast,' he breathed in a raw undertone. 'Because I'm a born and bred loner, Bunny. I don't do the couple thing. '

'Okay.' Bunny wasn't sure what she wanted. After Tristram, she had decided that it would be a long time until she got seriously involved with anyone again, had dimly pictured enjoying light, fun relationships.

But fate had instead thrown up Sebastian. The force of his personality could be overwhelming.

'I'm on fire for you.'

The very concept of being desired to that extent by Sebastian sent a naked flame racing through her bloodstream. But, just like him, she didn't want any big discussions or complications. There wasn't a nice, neat label for the attraction between them. Lust? She winced but maybe it was only that, yet so many other feelings surged in her in Sebastian's radius. He was so wary, so damaged, she sensed, and she wouldn't have been human had she not wanted to know why. It wasn't solely his experience with an unhappy girl who had fixated on him while he was still a boy, she reckoned.

'Fancy a swim?' she prompted abruptly.

Her suggestion broke the tension. On the beach, Sebastian stripped off everything and laughed when she got into the water in the shirt and the material ballooned up around her. 'Want to borrow my boxers?' he teased.

And she agonised over what she truly wanted because she wanted him, didn't even need to think about it. Did that mean that she was already too keen?

Was she asking for trouble when she already knew he was going to walk away? Or was she worrying about tomorrow when *today* was really all she should be concentrating on? A short-term future only, she decided. If she wanted him to back off, he would, but was that what she wanted? She didn't think so.

She watched him in the water, lithe as an otter, unexpectedly graceful for all his size. Backed by lush vegetation, the sunlit beach was sublime. In the distance a slender column of black smoke swirled up from the little bonfire. It hadn't attracted anyone's attention yet, she noted, nor had their painstakingly made SOS messages on the beach.

'You didn't finish the story. What happened to Ariana afterwards?' she asked.

'I haven't remembered that far back yet, but she did have another episode at university and she dropped out.'

Bunny grimaced as she leant back against the wooden pier. 'Why do you take on that guilt? You didn't cause her problems. I would assume she was troubled beforehand even if her family didn't realise that and families often don't. If it hadn't been you who became her focus, it would've been some other boy. It wasn't your fault.'

'It felt like it,' Sebastian countered grimly.

Bunny changed the subject. 'How much wood is there left to keep that bonfire going?'

'I'm reluctant to start felling trees,' he admitted. 'I don't want to do irreparable damage here. I've already combed through most of the undergrowth and removed logs. A nature lover like the owner of that house wouldn't like trees being felled.'

'When will you use the flares?'

'In a few days. I'm hoping we'll hear search planes. We've got to allow that time for a search to begin.'

He settled upright just in front of her and braced his big hands on the pier either side of her. Spectacular dark eyes gazed down into hers.

'You're remembering stuff,' she murmured. 'You're different.'

'How different?'

'More impatient, bossier...bouncing off the walls with surplus energy,' she muttered with rueful amusement.

'I don't like being in situations I can't control.'

'This experience could teach you patience.'

Disconcerting her, Sebastian turned away. 'I'll swim for a while, work off that energy.'

Her brow indented and then she dropped back into the water and swam back to shore.

What the hell was he doing with her? Sebastian was asking himself. She wasn't up to his weight. She wasn't fragile or lacking in confidence like Ariana though. She was her own woman and she didn't trust him. And why should she? Practising withdrawal as a means of contraception? *Really?* He knew how unreliable that was. What had possessed him? And why was he so drawn to her? He needed to give her some space and work out what was happening to him before it all blew up in his face. He wasn't himself, particularly with her. He felt that down to his very bones and the feeling unnerved him. Yet he still couldn't make himself step back from her.

Bunny went back to the house and, to keep occupied, changed the bed. The linen cupboard was full, as if waiting for a full house of guests, and yet there was only that one bed. She missed books. The few books on shelves were of the ornithology variety, not very tempting to someone like her who liked fiction and history. She located the cushions for the outside furniture in a cupboard and grabbed one to sit and survey the tiny view of the beach, which was mostly screened by trees that needed to be cut back. Eventually she dozed off, reflecting that she already missed Sebastian and that there was no way she was going to stop whatever they had started up. Life was simply too short to be that cautious of something or someone new.

'Time to eat,' Sebastian told her, shaking her shoulder.

'You...cooked?'

'Yes, and you're not allowed to criticise,' he warned her, herding her back into the house and the kitchen where he set a plate of pasta in front of her with a flourish.

Still waking up, she ate, deciding that Sebastian could be a little bit annoying because he was good at so many different things. The food was excellent, if spicier than she would have dared to make it.

'I'm going for a shower,' he told her while she was clearing up.

'I'll be in bed.'

He stalked back from the doorway and pulled her into his arms. 'Tell me I can kiss you.'

'You can do anything you like,' she murmured, lifting her head high, clear green eyes striking his levelly. 'And we're not about to stress about that any more.'

'Did it hurt when you fell from heaven?' he teased, dark-as-night eyes glittering like stars as his tension vanished.

For a split second, relief flooded him and he just wanted to grab her and whirl her round the kitchen. It was a weird urge and it knocked him off balance. Possibly he was more stressed than he had been willing to admit but resisting the urge to put his arms round her was still a challenge. Why was he getting these insane feelings of affection that had nothing whatsoever to do with sex? Why wasn't he exasperated with her for playing hot and cold? Why wasn't he offended that she had had to put so much thought into being with him? Had that ever happened to him before?

She groaned and laughed almost simultaneously at that corny line. Her big green eyes sparkled. His big hands cradling her cheeks, he kissed her, fast, hard and full of dark promise, making her shiver with anticipation. 'Later,' he husked with a brilliant smile.

Yes, he wanted her fiercely and she would let herself enjoy that, revel in being desired, truly desired for the very first time. In her one and only relationship, she had been a useful stopgap, a temporary convenience for student life, never the girlfriend Tristram had planned to stay with long term, for all he had once said that she was. After that experience, Sebastian's desire, his bluntness about what he did and didn't want were exceptionally appealing to her. He wasn't telling her any lies, he wasn't faking anything. He didn't want love or commitment. It was honest. They *had* no future! They were having a fling and, goodness knew, she was old enough to have a fling without agonising about it and beating herself up.

There was just something about her, Sebastian reflected in the shower. He wondered how long it would take him to persuade her into the shower with him. He smiled. Having the lights on had been a big enough deal for her. She could be shy. She took for ever to make major decisions, and sex was clearly a major decision for her. She could be impulsive, though, and when she was, she was incredibly sexy. At the same time, she didn't back down with him when he crossed or criticised her and he was beginning to appreciate that quiet, firm, non-combative peace she emanated when he got difficult. She was his polar opposite. So why did they work so well together?

He was volatile, had always been volatile and inclined to brood. He was a science geek and when he was a child his social skills had been abysmal. He wasn't a party person. He didn't do drugs or drink much. His family background had ensured that he knew enough to avoid the obvious pitfalls. He liked sex but he didn't like the complications it brought, the women who demanded more than he had to give, the women who wouldn't give him space to breathe. Thinking about it, and the very idea made him want to laugh at the insanity of it, he realised Bunny was probably his very first relationship.

He had had next to no relationship with the relatives who had sent him away from them rather than take him into their own homes and families. Even his parents had been distant in his memories of them. Nobody had ever got really close to him, certainly not a woman. He had never lived with a woman before, seen her day after day, looked for her when she wasn't there, eaten her cooking, cooked for her. It was scarily intimate, he acknowledged, the sort of set-up he usually avoided like the plague. That in mind, why was he still enjoying being with her? Why wasn't he keeping his distance?

Bunny slid into the cool bed and shivered and a moment later Sebastian rolled over and caught her to him. The heat of him infiltrated every inch of her and liquid warmth stirred between her thighs. Her fingers slid up into his damp hair, the curls of black hair on his chest abrading her tender nipples as his mouth came down on hers with a hunger that both shook and thrilled. She wasn't about to catch feelings for him, she swore to herself, she wasn't going to get attached. Yet deep down inside her a little voice whispered that she was lying to herself and that it was easy to decide to live wild and free, but it would be more of a challenge to hold to that goal.

CHAPTER SIX

'I COULD MAKE COOKIES,' Bunny bargained ten days later.

'Cookies aren't nutritious,' Sebastian countered, sliding a glance over her slender frame as she sat beside him on the pier with her legs dangling. Her delicate features had thinned because they were both losing weight and it worried him. 'Let's conserve the supplies we have.'

'Maybe not but cookies are comforting,' Bunny argued. 'I still remember making them with my grandmother.'

And without the smallest fanfare a sound rather like a click went off inside Sebastian's brain. Click... *his* grandmother, Loukia was dead. For a split second he felt sick as he remembered that. Bang, all of a sudden everything he had forgotten was back in his head where it belonged, everything clashing and crowding together in an ungodly cacophony of demands. Loukia, the will, the onslaught of his relatives and the torturous stress of the latest software he was fine-tuning for the market. Was it any wonder his memory had checked out on him? He hadn't *wanted* to remember what his life was like, had he?

'And then she passed and, six months later, my grandfather was gone as well. And Mum can't bake for peanuts, so I became the baker at home,' Bunny continued. 'I miss my family. I wouldn't admit that I was homesick the whole year I've been away and I wouldn't let them pay for me to fly home for Christmas because it would've left them short for other things. And now they'll be worrying about me, afraid that something bad has happened and I feel so guilty...'

Thee mou...what had he done? He had never been so irresponsible in his choice of a woman. How he had ended up with someone as unsuitable as Bunny in his bed was a mystery unless it was the sheer novelty of her that had drawn him. The optimistic freshness of the way she saw life, her perpetual, painful honesty, her overdeveloped conscience. The easy affection she offered, the wonderful calm at the heart of her that steadied him. The absolutely amazing sex. Long fingers tightening on the fishing rod, he turned to look at his companion, knowing that he would be judging himself for ever more if he hurt her. 'Go back in the shade...you're burning again,' he told her with the curtness of guilt-stricken concern. 'Your nose is pink.'

'What's wrong?' she asked instantly, alert to the edge honing his dark deep voice.

'I got the rest of my memory back. When you

mentioned your grandmother it all simply slid into place and it's sobering stuff,' he grated, checking out fleeting images inside his head and almost flinching from the fallout.

'Don't go back to being the guy you were on the boat,' she warned him ruefully.

'It's too late for that. I'm the guy I was on the boat but I'm also the guy you've been with here for the past two weeks. I'm *both*,' he underlined.

Bunny didn't want to think about him being both because she had loathed the first version of him that she had met. 'You sent up the last flare last night,' she reminded him, suddenly very keen to change the subject.

'Because we heard planes,' he pointed out.

'Only they didn't come near us.

'What did you remember?' she finally forced herself to ask.

'Everything. That my grandmother passed away last month and it's a few years since I worked as a doctor. I'm in tech development now. I created an anti-hacking security program called Pagekey, which is making me a fortune,' he spelt out quietly and with a significant lack of excitement at the recollection.

'I'm so sorry about your grandmother,' she said quietly. 'Why did you give up medicine?'

'I wasn't compassionate enough. I prefer machines to people. They're more reliable. And I suspect I only went for medicine because all my relatives said I'd never make the grade. Isn't that petty? Let's talk about something rather more relevant.'

'Like?'

'What are our plans if you are pregnant?' he framed softly, choosing the topic that now concerned him most. 'After this length of time, it's possible that you have conceived.'

'Is it? Either of us could be sterile. It doesn't really matter right now anyway, not until we're rescued,' she reasoned awkwardly. 'But I wouldn't want a termination. I'd raise the baby...but I suppose it would wreck my life. Of course, that's a stupid, narrow-minded thing to say.'

'I don't want a child of mine wrecking anyone's life,' Sebastian admitted with glacial candour and a chill ran down her spine.

'I only meant it would wreck all my plans in the short term,' Bunny rephrased immediately. 'My family would fuss and worry. It would mean planning a different future, that's all. Don't judge me for a first passing reaction to a possible crisis. And *don't* freeze me out!'

'I'm not.'

Bunny studied his breathtakingly beautiful face, the new reserve etched into his lean, dark, perfect features, the absence of his easy smile, the taut and wary narrowing of his stunning black-lashed eyes. And she saw the difference in him since he had regained his memory because he hid his emotions. 'You are and you know you are. I know you.'

'You don't. Not the way you think you do,' he assured her smoothly. 'We haven't been living a normal life here.'

'I still know that you want answers right now this minute and solutions at the same time,' she responded flatly. 'And we're not in a position to talk about either, so this is a futile conversation.'

In truth, she had summed up pretty much what he wanted and couldn't have and he almost laughed at how well she had him tabbed. But he didn't laugh because he knew that he needed to back off from the hothouse intensity of their current relationship.

'After this, I *will* walk away…but I won't walk away from my child, should there be one.'

'I'm going for a walk now,' Bunny told him tautly as she scrambled upright in a sudden movement. 'Oh…just one question…*did* you have a girlfriend?'

'No. When I met you, I hadn't been with a woman in months,' he countered.

'So glad I was available for you. Let's hope we'll be rescued soon and then we can escape each other,' she sniped, walking off fast, well aware that right now he would prefer his own company.

Sebastian liked his own space and he especially would dislike if she began shooting twenty questions at him in relation to his returned memories. But she shouldn't have been snide, she scolded herself in shame. If he had only just remembered his grandmother's death, he would be reliving that grief. She was being selfish and insensitive dwelling only on what the return of his memory would mean to her.

'I will walk away.'

What was she supposed to say to that? Could he have shouted the end to their relationship any louder?

He had changed. The minute he had remembered who he was, he had changed so fast her head was still spinning with the shock of it. Sebastian Pagonis, rich tech tycoon. Not a playboy though. She supposed that was a very small comfort. But even so, his very first urge had been to push her away, diminish what they had shared and make it clear that what they currently had was finished the moment they were rescued. Her eyes stung and she blinked furiously, sun glinting off the clear water almost blinding her in the afternoon heat. Her own response to his words made it clear that somewhere down deep she had been hoping that what they had was something more than a forgettable fling.

And now she was upset—well, that had always been on the cards, Sebastian reasoned grimly. If he wasn't prepared to offer the ring, the white picket fence and the family dog, she would be upset and there was nothing he could do about it. Bunny was deeply conventional and he had recognised that early on, so why hadn't he backed off then? A baby? He groaned and felt ashamed of the response. But what did he know about being a father? What did he even know about having a family? Yet he had taken risk after risk with Bunny and once or twice he had even forgotten to be careful. So the odds of her conceiving, when they had been in that bed every day since their arrival, could be pretty high.

Bunny dashed away the furious, over-emotional tears while she reminded herself that she needed to rewrite the last two weeks inside her head. Forget the fling, dial back the emotions, start treating Sebastian like a platonic companion, stop sharing the same bed and ditch all the little intimacies that had begun to seem so natural between them. Why? As he had reminded her, none of what they had shared while stranded was normal. Their life here *wasn't* normal, so how could anything that had grown from their situation be any different?

The distant drone of an engine was sufficient to penetrate her troubled thoughts. After all, they heard no mechanical sounds on the island. She looked back over her shoulder and saw Sebastian running down the beach and beyond him she saw some kind of boat noisily bouncing over the waves towards the island. It had finally happened. Someone had noticed their presence. Not quite able to credit that reality, she momentarily froze and then she began running in the same direction as well.

By the time she arrived, Sebastian was already enjoying an animated conversation with the man, who had tied up his motorboat at the pier. He paused and formally introduced her to Dwi, the caretaker for the 'French house', as it was described, and she noted that Sebastian seemed to speak quite a bit of Indonesian dialect. The owner was a guy named Louis Bernard, an ornithologist and a leading light in television documentaries. A mobile phone was handed to Sebastian with great ceremony.

'Dwi knows that we've been reported missing because it's all over the newspapers. I'm calling my friend Andreas so that the search can be called off. He'll organise everything for us and then I'm going to call Mr Bernard, so that I can explain that we broke into his house to use it. Reggie was picked up last week, by the way,' he advanced. 'But he's in hospital with an injured leg which requires surgery.'

The phone was passed back and forth for Dwi to give the exact location of the island. Sebastian spoke in Greek, laughing occasionally and smiling, and she surmised that Andreas was a close friend. They all began walking towards the house as Sebastian phoned the house owner to offer their thanks for its use as well as assurances that the house would be returned to its original state.

The phone was returned to Dwi. 'We'll be picked up this evening by helicopter,' Sebastian informed her. 'Your family are already waiting for you. My yacht arrived in Bali last week and I've told Andreas to invite your family to use it for the duration of their stay.'

'My family's here?' Bunny gasped in consternation. 'How many of them?'

'Parents and a couple of brothers, I believe,' Sebastian supplied.

'We can't stay on your...yacht,' she declared uncomfortably.

'Why would you put them to the expense of staying anywhere else?' Sebastian questioned with a frown.

A deep tide of red washed up over her heart-shaped face because that was unanswerable. Her parents were retired and would've dug deep into their savings to fly out to Indonesia. Anything that could lessen the cost of their unexpected stay in Asia would be welcome to them. 'You have a *yacht*?' she said instead of all the many more embarrassing things that she might have said without thinking.

Back in the real world, she was thinking, the differences between her and Sebastian were starkly apparent. He had a yacht! He spoke sufficient Indonesian to have soothed the anxious Dwi and he spoke French fluently while her grasp of the language had advanced no further than the exam she had passed at sixteen. 'I don't want to get on another boat,' she confessed uneasily.

'The yacht won't be sailing anywhere and it's the size of a small cruise ship.'

Bunny swallowed the lump in her throat and nodded obediently because she would have to get over her newly learned aversion to boats to allow her family to take advantage of Sebastian's hospitality. And *his* thoughtfulness on her family's behalf, her conscience slotted in, but she really didn't want to be reminded that Sebastian was that rich and important that his disappearance had been reported in newspapers. Or that, in spite of his wealth and influence, he could still be unexpectedly kind.

While the two men talked, Bunny's memory ranged free.

At dawn that morning, Sebastian had been studying her when she wakened and had informed her that the sun had given her a fifth freckle on her nose. 'So admit it, I notice everything about you,' he had teased, shifting over her, already hard and urgent against her. 'Now you have to say good morning *my* way...'

'Not until I've freshened up.'

'You smell of me and I find that stupendously sexy,' he had husked.

She had gloried in the sensation of having those stunning dark eyes of his locked to her. 'According to you, you find everything about me sexy.'

'So let me take advantage of you again...'

And without hesitation, they had taken advantage of each other, she conceded, her feminine core tingling in erotic recollection of that passion. Although she had not known it at the time, she reflected now, that had been their *last* time together. It was over, done, dusted, soon to be forgotten about, she told herself. She wasn't about to agonise over a stupid, meaningless fling. She wasn't that big an idiot!

For heaven's sake, why was she standing around

dreaming when they would soon be leaving? She needed to tidy the house, change the bedding, pick up her few belongings. As she sped indoors, Sebastian caught her by the elbow. 'We'll eat on the yacht.'

'Please tell me there'll be vegetables. You wouldn't believe how much I've missed them!' she sighed, rolling her eyes with determined cheer.

'I have a chef. You can choose your favourite meal,' he promised. 'Roasted veg and cheese? And a dessert?'

'I can hardly wait,' she said brightly, noting that he had tied up his hair again with a length of vine and that miraculously he already looked much more like the guy she had first met. Self-contained, rather remote, his brilliant dark eyes veiled even though his tone was light and casual.

'An official investigation has been opened into the wreck,' Sebastian warned her. 'We'll have to make statements to the police and the shipping authorities. You'll have to watch what you say or you could get Reggie into trouble because that mast should never have come down like that. Either they'll find a reason for it failing or they'll try to blame him for taking out a vessel that wasn't seaworthy.'

Bunny nodded very seriously. 'He wouldn't have done that.'

'No and luckily we're both in good health, which will help matters.'

'But you were hurt.'

'The mast caught the back of my head as it went

down. I was fortunate the effects weren't more serious.' Sebastian paused and studied her. 'Though I would ask you to keep my temporary amnesia a confidential matter. I'm over it. It's no longer relevant. Nobody else needs to know.'

His amnesia was not relevant and she suspected that in his view that covered their temporary relationship as well. 'Understood. I'm not going to talk about you to anyone,' she told him stiffly and turned away.

'There are people who will offer you a lot of money to tell them about your experiences with me here,' he cautioned her tautly. 'If that is likely to tempt you to talk, I would be happy to give you the cash upfront in return for your silence.'

Every scrap of colour evaporated from Bunny's complexion. 'I have no intention of selling you out, Sebastian. But it's interesting how immediately distrustful you've become since regaining your memory.' Bunny's green eyes were reproachful, her tone stiff. 'I may not be rich but I'm happy with what I've got and no matter what I'm offered, I won't be tempted to reveal any secrets that could embarrass you.'

She went upstairs to collect their few possessions and strip the bed.

'You don't need to bother,' Sebastian said from the doorway. 'Dwi says the owner is putting this place up for sale. Apparently, this was once his dream hideaway but he's since got married and his wife doesn't like being so far from civilisation, so he's not using it any more.'

'Even so, I'll put the sheets on to wash,' she murmured. 'It's the polite thing to do.'

She was keeping busy to avoid having to think about what Sebastian had revealed. He had just offered to pay her cash, to *bribe* her to prevent her from talking about her experiences on the island with him. Well, that told her all she needed to know about his opinion of her. Would he have believed ill of her as easily *before* he regained his memory? Was he always this cynical and suspicious? It occurred to her that perhaps she had been lucky to be washed up with a Sebastian who barely knew who he was. To say the least, the fully restored version of Sebastian inhabited a 'them' and 'us' world from which she, by virtue of her economic status, was excluded. He didn't trust her any more but maybe he had *never* trusted her.

It was cool and damp when she heard the helicopter overhead. The late summer weather was definitely on the turn. Although the days remained hot the evenings were getting cooler. As she stepped out of the house, she carried a small bundle and when she reached the beach, she tossed Sebastian's sweater at him.

Frowning, he turned to her.

'You forgot it!' she yelled above the racket of the helicopter settling down on the beach. It had a very sleek paint job in purple and silver and some sort of logo on it.

He strode back towards her. 'I left it for you… it's cold.'

'I'm fine.'

He ignored her assurance and instead ran a reproving finger over the goosebumps on her arm. He dropped his sweater over her head, feeding her hands carefully into the sleeves before stooping to lift her off her feet into his arms to carry her.

'What are you doing?' she demanded in astonishment.

'You don't have any shoes!' he vented in surprise at her reaction as they were approached by the two men who had jumped out of the helicopter. Both were staring and one of them was her eldest brother, John. Her face burned with self-consciousness.

'I'll take her from here,' John asserted, extending his arms to remove her from Sebastian's hold.

Sebastian, however, stood his ground and lifted an arrogant black brow. 'And you are?'

'This is my brother John,' Bunny proclaimed hurriedly.

Sebastian relaxed his hold and handed her over like a parcel. 'Sebastian Pagonis.'

'John Woods.'

'Where's Mum and Dad?' Bunny asked as John moved her into the helicopter.

'There wasn't enough space for more than two of us to fly out here and Mum and Dad are a bit overcome by all this and Mum didn't want to cry over you in front of people.'

'Oh,' Bunny mumbled as the other man leant back over the seat in front and introduced himself as Andreas Zervas. Sebastian's friend, she recalled, and then they were all donning headphones to drown out the noise of the helicopter and there was no further opportunity for conversation. Bunny gazed numbly out of the window as the craft swung in a turn above the island to head back out across the sea. And from that vantage point, the island looked absolutely tiny, the roof of the house only momentarily visible below the trees.

John grasped her hand and squeezed it. Tears prickled behind her lowered eyelids and her throat thickened. What a storm of drama and stress she had created for her family! John would have come without his wife and had probably travelled out to Indonesia with her middle brother, Luke, a corporate lawyer and the highest earner in the family.

It was a longer flight than she was expecting and she couldn't wait to see her parents and reassure them that she was perfectly all right. When the heavy craft finally set down again, she peered out of the window but she could see only technical equipment. She whipped off the headphones and John hissed in her ear, 'Wait until you see this boat...'

They had landed on the yacht? She was hugely relieved that no further travel was required to reach their destination and she moved down the steps onto the helipad, following Sebastian, who told her to watch her feet when she stubbed her toe and then, in exasperation, he lifted her up again. 'You need shoes!' he censured.

'If I hadn't been trying to help you onto the raft, I wouldn't have lost my shoe in the first place!' she snapped back with spirit, colouring when she noticed her brother's surprised glance.

Sebastian stalked through a door and lowered her to a rug. It was a huge reception area and at the very foot of it she saw her parents standing taut and somehow seeming very small against their imposing glass and opulently elegant surroundings. Bunny hurtled down the length of the room into her parents' arms. There was frantic speech and a lot of tears, questions that weren't answered and some harried answers that weren't entirely true. In the midst of it, Sebastian walked up to join them.

'She saved my life,' he told her parents and her brother Luke. 'She got me on the raft and looked after me until I'd recovered my wits.'

'And then he looked after me. He fished and built bonfires and dealt with snakes,' she recalled with a shudder.

Her mother wrapped her arms round Sebastian before Bunny could intercept her and gave him a huge, enthusiastic hug, only separating from him when Bunny's father insisted on shaking his hand while Bunny introduced everybody.

'Let me show you to your cabin,' Sebastian interposed. 'You'll want to get changed and catch up with your parents. I had Andreas organise some clothing basics for you.'

'Oh...er, thanks,' she muttered in a rush as he guided her across a companionway and into an utterly breath-stealing space before stepping out again, leaving her with her family. The cabin was almost as large as the reception area with a very opulent bed on a shallow dais, a snazzy separate seating area and doors out onto a deck. Another door stood ajar on a luxury bathroom that rejoiced in a copper tub, fleecy towels and glorious marble tiles.

'Wow...' Bunny whispered, impressed to death by her surroundings.

'The rest of us are on the deck below,' Luke imparted, frowning at her. 'He's put you next door to *his* cabin.'

Bunny investigated through the third door and rifled through a wardrobe packed with fluttering garments and drawers full of silky underwear. 'Well, I'm not about to complain about being spoiled after the last two weeks,' she confided, lifting her chin. Rather more than 'clothing basics' had been provided, she acknowledged, but she would take that up with Sebastian later in private.

'Of course she's not,' her mother piped up, shooting Luke a reproachful glance. 'Your sister's had a rough time.'

'Exactly how friendly are you with our generous host?' John enquired quietly.

Bunny shrugged. 'About as friendly as you would

expect after two weeks worried we weren't going to make it off that island any time soon,' she replied stiffly.

'That's not telling us anything,' Luke reproved.

'I don't owe you an explanation,' she heard herself say sharply and then her mother was shooing the men out, saying that she was overwrought and that it wasn't the time for a postmortem.

'You tend to get close when there's only the two of you all day every day,' she added apologetically as Luke departed with bad grace.

'Would you mind if I went for a shower and got dressed?' she asked her mother as she gathered underwear, a long silky skirt and a light top from the dressing room. 'I need to freshen up.'

'You've changed,' the older woman remarked, her brow furrowing. 'I'm not criticising. You're more confident. Naturally the experience you've had and a year away from home has changed you.'

Bunny stripped and sped into the shower, revelling in the shampoo and the conditioner for her hair and then dressing in haste, all fingers and thumbs as she combed her hair, ran a dryer through it and finally thrust her feet into leather sliders that must've cost the earth. The garments were classy and chic and pleasantly soft and silky against her skin. When she reappeared both her parents were in the seating area chatting and, minutes after that, a stewardess knocked on the door to say that dinner was about to be served.

'Only Bunny is having the roast vegetables because it's her favourite,' Sebastian announced, sending her a fleeting smile. He had changed as well but only into well-worn jeans that fitted his big muscular body as if they had been tailored for him and a loose white linen shirt, bright against his bronzed skin. He had shaved, his strong jawline exposed without the covering black stubble she had grown accustomed to seeing there. His amazing dark good looks had never been more obvious. His brilliant dark eyes gleamed as they rested on her with satisfaction.

'So looks like you've got very friendly with our host,' her brother Luke remarked, his hand at her spine to guide her into a chair at Sebastian's elbow and at a very long polished table.

Drinks were served first but Bunny was hungry enough that her tummy felt as though it were meeting her backbone and as soon as she was able she ate with appetite, cherishing the luxury touches of melted cheese and some sort of moreish chutney.

Most of the conversation centred on their escape during the storm and the island.

'Apparently the caretaker, Dwi, checks the house once a month and he spent the last few weeks away from home visiting relatives. His neighbour phoned him to say that he had seen smoke coming from the island but he didn't believe him. The neighbour was known for telling tall stories but that's why Dwi came out to the island today.'

Stifling a yawn, she cleared her plate. Several

times, Sebastian stepped in to answer questions because she was flagging and she wished he would quit his self-appointed role acting as her protector. Evidently, Reggie's catamaran had been saved but it was now official evidence and, bearing in mind his injury, it would probably be weeks, if not months, before his boat was returned to him. Her father had already visited his old friend in hospital and he told her that Reggie's wife, Eka, had been with him. Her family had waited several days after the alarm of her disappearance had been raised before deciding to fly to Indonesia because they had wanted to be on the spot if there were any developments during the search.

'You're exhausted,' Sebastian told her.

'Yes, but I'm too wired to go to sleep yet,' Bunny confided.

'Do you want to call it a night? Or would you like to join me for coffee?'

'Coffee,' Bunny selected.

'We'll have coffee on deck. Coffee with cream,' Sebastian said with a sudden grin and, for a moment, it was as though they were the only two people in the world. His spectacular dark eyes were bright as starshine and held hers fast.

'And biscuits?' she pressed hopefully.

'Play your cards right and there might even be a dessert. I told my chef that you had a sweet tooth.'

Even aware that her family were watching her like hawks, Bunny still let Sebastian draw her neatly away from the table and guide her towards the deck doors.

'Right now, you're overwhelmed,' Sebastian murmured soft and low. 'Too many people around you, too many questions at once. We were living on a very quiet island and we'll both need time to adjust to the change.'

Sometimes he got everything right, she conceded, but sometimes he got it dreadfully wrong: as when he had offered her money in an effort to persuade her not to discuss him with the press. As if she would ever have contemplated doing that! She shifted away from him and took a deeply upholstered seat behind a fancy table in a trendy S shape. She breathed in the sea air with surprising pleasure, seeing the lights of the Bali nightlife in the distance while reassured that the giant yacht would not be moving while she was onboard.

'How did you organise these clothes for me?'

'I told Andreas that you had nothing but a pair of pyjamas to wear and no shoes. I gave him your sizes. I assume his wife helped him,' he responded lazily as a stewardess appeared carrying a laden tray. 'Until you're reunited with whatever remains of your belongings on Reggie's catamaran, you have nothing. Anything you don't want or like from the selection will be returned. Tomorrow you'll be speaking to the police and the shipping investigators and I doubted that you would want to do it barefoot in pyjamas.'

'But the expense,' she protested uncomfortably,

only a little mollified by the news that some garments could be returned.

'I want you to be comfortable.'

'You're not responsible for me,' Bunny told him with curt conviction as she poured the coffee and sugared hers and added cream, cupping the warm brew between her palms to drink.

'I will be if you're pregnant.'

Her eyes flew to the deck doors, but the stewardess had closed them again and she turned back to him. 'No,' she corrected. 'You'll be jointly responsible for the baby once it is born...that is *if* there's a baby. You're not responsible for me in any other way.'

Sebastian dropped down beside her in an elegant careless sprawl, long legs sheathed in taut denim stretched out in front of him. 'You need to relax about this or we're going to be arguing constantly. I've organised a blood test for you tomorrow morning, so that we'll know whether or not we're about to become parents.'

'No,' Bunny countered quietly. 'When I do a pregnancy test I will choose the time and the place and I'm not ready to cross that bridge yet. Anyway, it's too soon.'

'No, it's not and the sooner we know, the better.' Sebastian closed a big hand over hers where it was clenched tight on the table top. 'Stop burying your head in the sand.'

'I'm not but I won't be railroaded into something I don't want.' She finished the biscuit, which had turned to sawdust inside her mouth, and stood up. 'I'm never likely to be a fan of you taking charge of everything—even stuff that isn't, strictly speaking, any of your business. But as far as you're concerned, if I'm pregnant, the baby doesn't exist until it's born and everything prior to that is totally *my* private business.'

Sebastian caught her hand to tug her down on his lap before she could move out of reach and a startled little gasp of dismay parted her lips. 'What are you doing?' she demanded, taken by surprise and struggling to rise off his lean, muscular thighs again.

Long fingers tipped up her chin, his gaze collided with her angry green eyes. 'Isn't it obvious?'

Sparks were flaring in his dark eyes and yet when his mouth came down and ravished hers, it was tantalisingly sweet and sensually tender. Her body ignited, programmed, it seemed, to still respond to him. Her nipples were tight, her breasts swelling, her breath ragged and the space between her thighs ached. But she lifted her hands and thrust them hard against his shoulders to push him back and detach herself.

'*No!*' she told him fiercely as she scrambled awkwardly and clumsily upright again, grasping the edge of the table to steady herself.

'No?' Sebastian queried in apparent surprise, which inflamed her even more.

'*That* is the past, this is the present. We had a fling and now it's done. Nobody was more blunt than you about the fact that we were over the minute we got off the island!' she reminded him. 'You said you would be walking away...well, I *walked* too, Sebastian. And after you offered to bribe me not to talk about you to the press, I didn't just mentally walk. I freakin' sprinted in the opposite direction!'

Faint colour darkened his blade-sharp cheekbones but his bright dark eyes flashed like lasers against the night sky. 'So, we're done...but how can we be if you're preg—?'

'I can be the mother of your child without that including any further intimacy. You know what the real problem is?' Bunny prompted furiously. 'It's *you*, naturally devious and twisty, suspicious you. If I'd clung to you and tried to attach strings, you'd be at the far end of your stupid pretentious yacht right now, *avoiding* me like the plague! But I didn't cling and because I chose to move on fast, now you're offended.'

'I'm *not* offended,' Sebastian grated in raw interruption.

Bunny rolled her eyes because he was totally offended by her rejection. 'I'm going to turn in now, because if I stay we're going to fight.'

'You'd back down before it got that far.'

In a real temper now, Bunny planted her hands on her hips. 'No, I wouldn't. Why can't you decide what you want? You said you were walking away... why aren't you?'

Sebastian shrugged a wide shoulder. He couldn't answer that question and he admired her in silence.

He still wanted her, the same way he had wanted her the day before and the day before that. His need to keep her close only intensified around other people and that was a shock to his system while landing him on unfamiliar ground. He had believed he could walk away and had discovered different. Even the prospect of her moving out of his sight set his teeth on edge. It wasn't logical and it disturbed him, but he couldn't escape those feelings, those urges.

In addition, it astonished him that he had once written her off as merely pretty, because, even without making the smallest effort, she was beautiful. Golden hair shining beneath the lights, her delicate face flushed, green eyes ablaze, soft pink lips lusciously full, her slender little body taut with tension. She was as addictive as a drug. He got within a yard of her and all he wanted to do was pin her to the nearest horizontal surface, *touch* her, *hold* her. That need was a complete novelty to him. No other woman had ever had that effect on him.

'I can't walk away if you've conceived,' he reminded her, wondering why it had become so important that he kept her close. Habit from the island? Had he become attached to her in some way? He didn't get close to women, yet the prospect of even going to bed *without* Bunny was a new challenge.

'No, but you can back off until the baby's born… if there is one,' she said drily.

'Is that what you want?'

'Yes, in the circumstances it would be wiser,' she

said stiffly. 'We both have to move on. I'll inform you if I have any news to share.'

'Okay.' Sebastian heard himself agree to what he didn't want and he was troubled by the knowledge. Being reasonable struck him as a fool's game. Yet logic sat at the very heart of him and he could not understand his own behaviour. For some reason he didn't feel logical about Bunny. What he wanted he didn't want to label.

Her brothers walked her back to her cabin and joined her inside without invitation. 'Has he asked you to sign an NDA?' Luke asked. 'He's asked us and we agreed because we're staying on this yacht.'

'No, he hasn't asked me yet but I'll probably say no,' Bunny admitted. 'I've no plans to talk about him but it was my experience too and I will retain the rights to my side of it.'

John grimaced. 'He's very possessive of you. Are you involved with him?'

Bunny sighed. 'I *was* but it's over now.' She had no intention whatsoever of getting into the possibility of her being pregnant and decided to shelve that for another day.

Her eldest brother looked relieved. 'That's probably for the best. I'm no pop psychologist but, with his background, he's got to be messed up to some degree.'

Bunny held her breath, waiting for him to elaborate but he didn't, and she watched her brothers depart in frustration. She got ready for bed, paced the floor, wondering what her feelings were for Sebastian. Whatever, those emotions were powerful and she *had* to know why he might be messed up. She didn't want anyone else's slant on his secrets either, nor, once she had the means to do so, did she want to look him up online, but the idea of snooping struck her as disrespectful.

She tiptoed to the cabin across from hers and gently rapped on the door. It was abruptly answered, swinging wide on a bare-chested Sebastian, barefoot and clad only in his jeans. 'Yes?'

'Sorry to interrupt but I wanted to know why your background might have messed you up...'

Sebastian blinked and then studied her intently. 'Someone's been talking.'

Reproach in her luminous gaze, she murmured drily, 'But not you...'

Without warning, he flung the door wide and stepped back. Lean bronzed muscles rippled as he shifted uneasily. 'You've got a nerve expecting answers after what you said earlier.'

Bunny winced in agreement. 'I don't want to look you up on the Internet and pry.'

A grim laugh was wrenched from his compressed lips. 'Even if that is what everyone else does?'

Bunny nodded in confirmation and stepped over the threshold.

CHAPTER SEVEN

IT WAS TIME that he told her about his back story, Sebastian reasoned heavily. He preferred to tell it in his own words rather than leave it to her to read the dramatic horrors online.

'It's bad stuff,' he warned her.

'I'm a good listener.'

'My grandmother indulged her eldest son, Jason, in every way,' Sebastian imparted wryly. 'He was the apple of her eye, no matter what he did, and when he met my mother, she was equally spoiled and wilful. Together they were a disaster but they married and had me. People thought it was a good match because they were both very rich. But my father never settled down. He was heavily into drugs and eventually my mother turned to other men.'

'Oh, dear...' Bunny mumbled, watching him pour himself a drink on the other side of the cabin.

'Do you want anything?' he asked.

'Water,' she chose, eying the lines of strain grooved round his wide sensual mouth, moving forward to accept the glass from him, belatedly guilty that she had cornered him into telling her what he so obviously didn't *want* to tell her. 'I'm sorry, I shouldn't have pushed you on such personal issues.'

Sebastian lifted her up with firm hands and deposited her on the end of the giant bed. 'You might as well know the facts when everyone else does,' he parried. 'In his twisted obsessive way my father adored my mother, but she'd met someone else and she insisted on a divorce. The lawyers who represented them were soon at each other's throats.'

'What age were you when all this was happening?'

'Six. The divorce fighting went on for months until one day my father just cracked. He'd already moved out of our home but when he arrived one evening, my nanny let him in,' he explained. 'It was her night off. As she left, my mother called the police. They started to argue and I hid behind the sofa. And without any warning—or indeed any prior record of violence—my father pulled out a gun and shot her...'

Bunny stared back at him with wide, horrified eyes.

'He was off his head. He was spraying bullets everywhere, stopping to reload, and then there was this silence for a long time. I was too scared to come out of hiding.' Sebastian was very pale, his lean, dark, perfect features taut as a bowstring in the lamplight. 'I heard one more shot...my father turned the gun on himself. The police found me with them. I was very distressed.'

Bunny stumbled off the bed and went over to him

to wrap both arms round him in a hug. 'I am *so* sorry that I forced you to relive that.'

Sebastian gazed down at her, disconcerted by her unhidden desire to comfort him. Something clenched tight in his chest and he set her back from him with newly learned circumspection. 'You'd better head to bed before your family find you missing. I'll see you in the morning.'

Bunny had never wanted so badly to stay with him but he had lived over twenty years with that tragedy and what could she offer him? Pale and taut, she headed back in shock from what she had learned. He must've been traumatised by such an ordeal and the simultaneous loss of both parents. Had his grandmother taken him in and brought him up? She assumed that Loukia, whom he had mentioned with such affection, must've done. What a ghastly past to have to live down, she reflected, shaken even more by that story of his than she had shown him.

She got into bed, reminding herself that, now that she and Sebastian were no longer involved, his upsetting background wasn't anything to do with her any more. So, why did she feel so agonised on his behalf? Why more than anything else in the world did she want to go back to Sebastian and keep on holding him? The time to express that kind of compassion and affection was already behind them. But, she acknowledged, her heart still yearned for him and the closeness they had enjoyed on the island without criticism or watching eyes judging them.

For goodness' sake, why was she thinking like a lovestruck teenager? Two weeks wasn't enough time to fall in love with anyone, she told herself. Love at first sight, well, it certainly hadn't been that. Lust and loathing at first sight, she reasoned, her entire body overheating with shame. And then from that first night when in truth she had thrown herself at him, other bonds had formed quite naturally. She had felt safe with him, she had trusted him, which was ironic when she reckoned that Sebastian did not trust anyone unless they came with a signed NDA.

She had never felt the way she felt now about Tristram. Neither that instant, unreasoning craving and the frightening power of it, nor the strong, deeper emotions constantly pulling at her. Falling for Tristram had been a slow, steady thing, wholly in keeping with her cautious, sensible nature. Falling for Sebastian was like falling into the eye of a storm.

She was neither cautious nor sensible about Sebastian. She had flung herself into his arms with no thought of a future and had assured herself that she could handle a temporary fling. Only now here she was and she wasn't handling the end of their relationship well, was she? But she had to bury her feelings and deal with the future, most especially if she had conceived.

Sebastian had always made it crystal clear that there was no tomorrow for them. He preferred being alone and he didn't engage in committed relationships with women. He didn't believe in happy marriages either and only now could she comprehend that he was damaged by living through his parents' unhappy marriage and its even more traumatic conclusion. But she had to accept all that and the impossibility of being with Sebastian ever again while at the same time embracing her own probably very different future. And if she *did* prove to be pregnant, would she and Sebastian eventually manage to become reasonably friendly co-parents?

And even worse, in the aftermath of his own ghastly childhood experience, how would Sebastian feel about becoming a parent? Clearly, he had suffered from his parents' troubled marriage. She wouldn't be a bit surprised to learn that Sebastian had never planned to father a child.

'You look beautiful,' Sebastian said with unexpected warmth over the breakfast table.

Disconcerted by that unexpected compliment concerning the plain green sun dress and flat canvas shoes she wore, Bunny smiled back at him, ignoring the sudden telling break in her family's conversation as every eye turned to them. 'Thanks,' she said simply.

'We're leaving for the police station in half an hour and we'll follow that up with the shipping team interview.'

'I'd like to visit Reggie in hospital if that's possible. After all, I won't see him again once I go home...

and he was good to me. It was only a few weeks but he was a great boss.'

Her father leant across the table to say, 'Did your mother tell you about Tristram turning up on our doorstep?'

Bunny froze. '*Tristram?* Why on earth would he call with you?'

'He read about you going missing in the newspaper and came to us to ask if there was any news or if there was anything that he could do to help,' her mother explained. 'We didn't invite him in. He left his number but I shouldn't think any of us will be making use of it.'

'The nerve of him! It's not as if we parted as friends,' Bunny exclaimed in a combination of annoyance and resentment, for she had neither seen nor spoken to her ex-boyfriend in a long time. To say the least, their breakup had been messy.

'He's still allowed to be concerned over whether you're alive or dead,' John declared mildly.

Sebastian brooded at the suspicion that the ex-boyfriend was hovering and awaiting Bunny's return. He was annoyed that she had refused the immediate blood test that would've told them whether or not there was going to be a baby but, whether he liked it or not, it was her body and her choice. He needed to get out of the habit of trying to intervene and boss her around because she didn't like it. She didn't suffer from his impatience, his need to plan every step in advance and to always know exactly where he was going. Well, she had killed those goals stone dead the same moment she came into his life, he reckoned with grim humour. He didn't know what he was doing, what he was planning to do next, no, he *only* knew that he wanted her.

He had told her that he would walk away. He had believed that he would walk away. He had been wrong. Still wanting her felt obsessional and it unnerved him. Moderation was always his rule with women but there was nothing moderate about the way he felt. From that first night on the island she had felt like *his* in some primal, utterly inexplicable and absurd way. And he had grown attached to that sensation as if some vital part of him had awakened, had changed him, had turned him inside out and upside down, subjecting him to extreme irrational urges. It was unnerving and he had to get a grip on it fast. He had to let her go, he had to let her walk away…for a time, at least. He had to give her the space to catch her breath before he pressed her.

Bunny was ill at ease because Sebastian was quiet, perfectly polite and pleasant when he did speak but mentally miles away. They got into the helicopter, only the two of them because it was only them who had to give statements and answer questions. From the moment they disembarked at the airport to travel by car into the city, they were surrounded by a security team, who prevented the cameramen and the journalists from either photographing them or questioning them.

'I didn't realise that it would be like this,' Bunny admitted, shaken by the excitement that their arrival had caused and the heaving desperation of the press to get closer to them.

'I've arranged for an official statement to be made about our rescue, but they want the whole story and they're not going to get it,' he responded curtly.

Within an hour they were inside the police station and making their statements, an Indonesian lawyer who apparently worked for Sebastian overseeing every step. It was shocking to witness how much attention and deference Sebastian received simply by dint of being an extremely wealthy and powerful tycoon. On the other side of the city, they answered the investigators' questions about the night of the storm, Reggie's actions and what the two of them had seen and done.

Soon afterwards they were visiting the older man in hospital, where he was now recuperating from his surgery. Reggie explained that a tiny fracture had been found in the mast, the result of a collision with another boat months earlier. At the time the authorities had judged the catamaran undamaged.

They wished him well and returned to the yacht, where she found her family packing up to leave.

'We assume that you have to stay another few days to satisfy the officials,' her father told her ruefully. 'But, lovely as it is here, we need to get home and your brothers need to get back to work.'

'You don't need to stay on in Indonesia and neither do I,' Sebastian told Bunny stiffly, fighting his own inclinations to retain her to the last ditch. 'Any further queries will be passed to us or dealt with by my legal reps here. You can travel home with your family today.'

Shock forked through Bunny like lightning and she turned pale. 'But I haven't got my stuff back yet,' she mumbled weakly.

'It'll be sent on to you once it's made available. I did take the liberty of finding you a spare phone,' Sebastian added, handing her a brand-new mobile phone. 'I put my number in there so that you can stay in touch.'

'Thanks...of course,' she mumbled, pale lips compressed at the prospect of leaving him, of possibly never ever seeing him again. 'I hope I still have a new job to start but who knows if they've held it open for me?'

Her mother wrapped a supportive arm round her. 'I'm so glad you're returning with us. The sooner you get back to a normal routine, the better you will feel.'

Bunny couldn't imagine a normal routine at home because she hadn't had one of those since childhood. She had only just moved home after completing her degree before she'd set off on her year of travel. Everything changed, nothing stayed the same and she looked up at Sebastian as if in appeal.

'It will be a welcome break from me,' he said quietly.

Bunny studied him, tracing those tantalisingly

beautiful dark male features and mentally kicking herself. She dropped her gaze in haste. No doubt he was in need of a break from her and he was right, there was no reason for her to stay on. She needed to get on with her life and leave him to enjoy his alone, the way he liked it. No clinging, no sighing, no tears, no excuses. She went back to the cabin and packed only what she had worn. At the very last moment, she picked up Sebastian's discarded Dior sweater, buried her nose in it, drank in the faint lingering scent of him and guiltily shoved it in the flight bag her mother had given her to use.

There it was: the result from the *third* pregnancy test and it was another positive.

Light-headed, Bunny left the cloakroom and got back to packing the library van with fresh books and special requests. On one level it annoyed her that Sebastian had been proven right to be convinced that she would be pregnant. She had thought that an unnecessarily pessimistic outlook, had been tempted to tell him that some women took for ever trying to get pregnant and that the likelihood of her conceiving after just two weeks of sex was slim.

Only now all she could recall was the sheer amount of sex they had had, the barriers that had fallen so fast when they were together all day and alone. It all flooded back into her memory: the spicy kitchen encounters, the swimming sessions, the times up against the walls, the doors. Face burning, she reckoned it would be true to say that Sebastian might as well have been chasing an Olympic record and that it would be unjust to blame him when she had been such a willing partner. The wild freedom of such intimacy had been new and crazily seductive to her and Sebastian's lack of inhibition had smashed down her boundaries one by one.

And now there was to be a baby. She was going to have a baby. A split second later she was smiling ear to ear because she mightn't have Sebastian but she would have his child. But how would *he* feel about that reality? Her smile died, the brief bubbly happiness that had blossomed inside her draining away. He didn't want a family. She had guessed that. On his terms, it would be the worst possible news.

'Aren't you away yet, Bunny dear? Been day-dreaming again?' her middle-aged boss enquired, popping her head into the van. 'If you don't watch out you'll be late for the stop at Little Moseby and there'll be complaints and then you'll be running behind all day.'

'I'm leaving right now,' Bunny asserted, deciding to text Sebastian at her first stop before she got into any more trouble.

She worked with two very nice ladies but saw little of them because she was always out with the library van touring rural areas, a service that those without transport very much appreciated. Her job had been held open and her late arrival forgiven because nobody had fancied the hassle of readvertising her position, although she was well aware that her colleagues felt that a man would have been a better fit for the post. It wasn't that anyone was being sexist, merely that they had assumed a man would be safer in lonely places and better able to handle the van when it broke down. They had yet to meet men like her brothers, who struggled even to change a tyre.

Once the rush of customers had tailed off in Little Moseby, Bunny pulled out her phone. It was six weeks since she had seen Sebastian. She had received her rucksack back and had texted him with her thanks, only it had not been the start of much of a conversation. He had asked how she was, the polite stuff, and, of course, she hadn't told him the truth because he wouldn't want to hear it. She was miserable, but she couldn't tell him that, couldn't tell him that her much-wanted job wasn't at all what she had imagined it would be and that living back at home was stifling. He had also sent her flowers every week, which had raised hopes that went unfulfilled because he had neither phoned to speak to her nor suggested that they should meet up.

'You fell for him,' her mother had sighed on that very long flight back home. 'Of course you did. He's very handsome and successful and all that stuff, but I expect it's not likely to go any further with him living in such a different world.'

She texted him, deciding to keep it bald and honest.

I'm pregnant.

She was on her third stop of the day by the time she got a response.

What did the doctor say?

I haven't seen a doctor. I did THREE tests.

Sebastian remained unimpressed.

Biting her lip, she typed that it would take days for her to get a doctor's appointment and that her brother worked in the surgery and that everyone would be put in an awkward, embarrassing position.

Sebastian wondered if she hadn't seen a doctor because she preferred to conceal her pregnancy and her past intimacy with him.

Are you ashamed of your condition?

He was clearly furious at that suspicion.

And that was it.

She almost threw her phone, the one he had bought her, through the windscreen in her rage with him. She didn't respond. Her phone kept on beeping with incoming texts and she ignored it. Sebastian was so particular about the details of absolutely everything. Every P and Q had to be minded and every T crossed. Sometimes he infuriated her and she wasn't dealing with that when she was supposed to be working. She just didn't want to let her family know that she was expecting until she had talked to Sebastian.

As if she didn't already know that she was pregnant even before she did those stupid tests, she thought wearily as she drove home in her mother's ancient car. Her menstrual cycle had stopped dead. Her breasts were sore. She was unbelievably tired and nauseous, and her sister-in-law, John's wife, Betsy, had experienced all those symptoms only months earlier. Unfortunately, however, the much-anticipated event of the first Woods grandchild had come to nothing when Betsy had had an early miscarriage. Currently pregnancy was a topic best avoided in the family.

As she parked her mother's car, she checked her texts, noting Sebastian's increasing frustration with her until the final text when he announced that he would be visiting her the next day.

She phoned him for the first time. 'You *can't*. I'm working all day.'

'I'll track down the library van and ambush you,' Sebastian said with remarkable good cheer.

'You're not...furious?' she prompted.

'No. I was expecting this development.'

Whoa, baby, don't get excited but you're a *development*. She rested her hand against her flat stomach and a feeling of warmth filled her.

'I'll organise lunch somewhere,' Sebastian told her briskly.

'I don't get very long...oh, it's a Friday,' she recalled abstractedly. 'I get longer for lunch on Fridays because it fits the itinerary better.'

'Wonderful. I'll see you around noon tomorrow.'

Right, well, that got the necessity of telling Sebastian out of the way. She screened a yawn in the hallway of the comfortable, cluttered bungalow where her parents lived. As she wandered into the kitchen to help her mother make dinner, she was wondering what she would wear the next day. Her last chance to impress before she lost her normal shape and started sprouting curves.

'Sebastian's coming down tomorrow to take me for lunch,' she revealed, looking on that admission as required footwork in advance of the more shocking revelation that she had conceived by a man who would have not the smallest intention or interest in putting a ring on her finger.

'Has something happened?' her mother enquired. 'I thought you weren't planning to see him again.'

'I didn't think I would get the chance,' Bunny said truthfully. 'But we have some stuff to talk about.'

'He's not sending you those extravagant flowers every week for nothing,' her father commented drily. 'Obviously he's still interested in you.'

Bunny tensed. 'Sort of... I think,' she parried uncomfortably.

'He's got a tragic back history but I wouldn't hold that against him,' her father, a retired policeman, said thoughtfully.

'I just don't want you to get hurt,' her mother chipped in.

And after dinner, unable to settle, Bunny told herself that she wouldn't get hurt even though she was already counting down the hours to seeing him again, picturing him, wondering how he would feel seeing her again. Would he feel *anything*? Bunny had never been more wretched than she had been for the past six weeks, missing Sebastian with every breath that she drew. The colour was leached out of her days by the giant black hole of unhappiness inside her. She had told herself that she didn't love him, that she hadn't known him well enough or long enough for love, but, in her heart, she knew that was a lie. For whatever reasons she had fallen for Sebastian Pagonis like a giant ton of bricks pitched off a cliff and having to get by without him weighed on her very heavily.

Sebastian appeared not long after she arrived at her last morning stop. She was busy tidying the shelves and checking the returns when she heard steps and she suppressed a groan because she assumed it was another customer. Instead, when she whirled round she was confronted by Sebastian, impossibly tall and broad and wholly unfamiliar in a very snazzy dark suit. She sucked in a stark breath, her heartbeat thundering.

'I'm a little early.'

'No, that's fine,' she said breathlessly. 'I just have to park the van in the pub car park and I'm free. You're looking very…tailored and elegant today.'

Sebastian gave her his lazy grin. 'I thought I should make an effort for once. I usually dress very casually.'

'Should I be flattered?' she teased. 'Or intimidated?'

'Hopefully not the latter,' he intoned in his smooth, well-bred drawl. 'Just don't be expecting it all the time.'

A huge smile lit up Bunny's face because she thought it was promising that he was already assuming that he would see her again. He looked amazing, black hair in his usual sleek style on top of his handsome head, and he really had gone to town on his appearance because he had teamed the suit with a silver-grey shirt and a red silk tie. Drop-dead gorgeous but never to be hers. Live in the moment, she urged herself, enjoy him for what he is, a luxury and a pleasure. But, ultimately, too rich for her blood.

'Shall we go?' he enquired, supremely proud of himself for not commenting on the fact that she looked as if she had lost weight and wasn't sleeping well. In fact, she seemed fragile, still beautiful though with her delicate face, snub nose and soft mouth, with her glorious golden hair tumbling round her narrow shoulders.

'I'll park the van...' With difficulty she dredged her gaze from him, her colour high, and closed the door to climb into the driver's seat.

When she'd finished locking up, she smoothed down her plain green dress, straightened her cardigan and tidied her hair, wincing because she owned not a single garment smart enough to impress anybody. It would take time and cash to build up a decent working wardrobe. Sebastian was posed beside a sleek sports car and another two cars were parked behind him, having already disgorged their occupants. Men in smart suits and earpieces were all over the place.

'Travelling in style?' she asked.

'The security?' He shrugged a broad shoulder as he ushered her into the passenger seat. 'No, this is the norm for me. My week in Indonesia was an escape week from these trappings and it turned into two weeks of freedom, so I'm not complaining.'

'Have you always lived like this?'

Sebastian swung into the seat beside her and ignited the engine. 'Pretty much for the last ten years.'

'We could have a quick meal at the pub here,' she pointed out.

'I wanted something more special.'

'Oh?' But Sebastian being Sebastian, he didn't take the bait or explain why he was opting for special rather than convenient.

A lean brown hand settled on her slender thigh briefly and she was tempted to put her hand down on top of his, eager for that connection and fighting the desire to deepen it. 'I missed having you around,' he told her. 'What's it like being back with your family?'

Her thigh tingled where he retained contact and then he removed his hand again, killing the buzz she had experienced. 'Pros and cons. I'd like to move out but I don't have a car and—' Suddenly conscious that she was lamenting her financial status to a billionaire, she winced inwardly. 'Well, there's just good reasons to live at home for the moment.'

'I've a feeling that that will change.'

'With me being pregnant?' Bunny shook her head as he filtered his silver Lamborghini down a long lane lined with wonderfully colourful maple trees. 'My family aren't the type to throw me out in the winter snow. Lecture me, maybe, be disappointed, probably, but nothing worse.'

'No, not that,' he said evasively as he pulled the car to a halt below the trees and parked in front of a long traditional farmhouse. 'This is a very exclusive restaurant. I hope it lives up to its ratings.'

'After the island I can eat anything, except not fish...please, no more fish for at least six months,' she pleaded as he climbed out, urging her to remain seated, and walked right round the bonnet to open her door for her. 'What are you doing?'

'Acting like a gentleman. You're pregnant,' he reminded her as he grasped her hand and lifted her gently out. 'You shouldn't be straining a single muscle right now.'

'You told me that you were raised to be a gentleman but that you don't behave like one,' she reminded him.

'I'm also highly adaptable. All my life, I've had to be,' he imparted, leading her through the parked cars, not to the front entrance as she had expected, but to a quieter side entrance. She heard the distant hum of voices and the clatter of china and cutlery. An older man greeted them and ushered them along a cosy panelled corridor into a very comfortable room with a beautifully set single table, two chairs and a big, cushioned sofa by the window. The fire in the old-fashioned fireplace was lit to ward off the autumn chill and decorated with pumpkin lights.

'This is lovely, very seasonal,' Bunny said warmly as they ordered drinks and the menus were presented. They both chose light bites rather than full meals. A private lunch date where they had their own room was unexpected but she assumed that once again Sebastian was conserving his privacy.

Sebastian fingered the tiny box in his pocket and breathed in deep. The server left the room. Sebastian looked at Bunny's happy smiling face with satisfaction and then he rose upright before dropping down fluidly onto one knee. He was being traditional so he might as well go the whole hog, he decided with determination, even if his agile brain was already throwing up a cartoonish image of the old-fashioned gesture. He clicked open the box and extended it and said with all the gravity he could muster, 'Will you marry me?'

CHAPTER EIGHT

BUNNY HAD NEVER been as shocked or unprepared for a surprise in her life. She leapt upright, wide-eyed and conscience-stricken. 'Oh, *no*!' she exclaimed in dismay. 'Please don't say anything more!'

Slanted ebony brows pleating in confusion, Sebastian slowly rose back to his feet and stared down at her in disbelief. 'I wasn't expecting you to immediately say yes but I did think you would be pleased. Instead, you're staring at me as if I asked something untenable!'

'Please sit down,' she urged shakily. 'Can I see the ring? Just out of sheer curiosity?'

Sebastian set the tiny box on the table. Bunny's eyes were stinging, pain and guilt and a whole host of other emotions swimming around inside her and threatening to spill over into the tears that were all too ready to assail her in recent times. She didn't need a doctor to tell her that her hormones were all roaring into pregnancy hyperdrive.

The ring was a glorious glittering diamond surrounded by emeralds in an art deco geometric shape. 'It's gorgeous,' she whispered admiringly.

'Did I say something wrong?' Sebastian demanded in a raw undertone.

'Sit down,' Bunny urged. 'I get dizzy when you stand over me.'

Lean bronzed profile taut, Sebastian sat back down in his seat.

Bunny leant forward and immediately reached for both of his hands. 'You *know* that you don't really want to marry me.'

'I beg your pardon,' Sebastian challenged, sculpted jaw determined.

She squeezed his hands as if to demand his full attention. 'Sebastian, I know how you feel about marriage. You don't believe in it or in relationships or in couples or in love. Let's talk plainly here,' she murmured steadily. 'You're asking me to marry you either because you think you *should* because I'm pregnant or because you think it's what I want and expect.'

'Thank you for clarifying that for me.' Sebastian spoke with sardonic bite.

'I never thought you would be so impulsive.'

'I miss you,' he framed in a driven undertone. 'It's been six blasted weeks. I'm not being impulsive, I'm being practical.'

'Practical isn't proposing to a woman you were only with for two weeks.'

'Two weeks, twenty-four-seven,' he incised the reminder.

'Marrying me would be a mistake for you. You don't want to be trapped into something like that,' she reasoned uneasily, a warm spot inside her spreading at his admission that he had missed her, had counted their weeks apart. 'We could end up hating each other by the time this baby's born, and splitting up always creates bad feelings, so co-parenting would be more difficult after a divorce.'

'And to think that I believed you were Little Miss Sunshine and yet you have made only negative assumptions about me and what I could offer.'

'You said you missed me...' Bunny hesitated and then bravely pushed herself on to go out on a limb and spell it out. 'Are you saying that you have feelings for me?'

She was literally hanging by her fingernails in the hope of an encouraging answer because that would have been a game-changer.

Instead, in a frustrated movement, Sebastian yanked his hands free of hers. 'No, I'm not. I'm *not* in love with you. I've never been in love and I don't want to be. Love can be a nasty, twisted thing and I want nothing to do with it. But I do believe that I can love my child and that my child can love me. If we're not together, though, I'll hardly see that child and that worries me. I also find the idea of being parted from you while you're carrying my baby even more worrying. I feel very strongly that we should be together *now*.'

Just for a moment, Bunny allowed herself to imagine how she would have felt if Sebastian had answered her differently, if he'd thrown out a few flattering lies and sprinkled them with stardust. Had he done that, she'd have bitten his hand off with eagerness to accept his proposal, but that wasn't Sebastian's way. He preferred brutal honesty. He didn't make empty promises or feed her half-truths with a sting in their tail, like Tristram insisting that he loved her even after she found him with another girl and then telling her while she was packing up to leave him that she was boring and dull in bed.

'You're not prepared to marry me and take a chance on me, are you?' Sebastian breathed in an almost savage undertone.

'Not right now. It's too soon and I'm not convinced you've thought it through in enough depth. I can imagine nothing worse than becoming your wife and then you changing your mind about wanting to be married.' Well, actually she could, she reflected reluctantly. Sebastian walking away for ever would be the absolute worst scenario. And he would probably never ask her to marry him again and that was a thought that made her feel a little desperate and fear that she was her own worst enemy.

'We could get engaged,' she suggested in a sudden rush. 'Try that for size first.'

Sebastian was too restive to stay still and he was pacing the small room, swinging back abruptly to her to say, 'You'd agree to that option?'

'Why not?'

'We'd have to live together,' he told her without

hesitation. 'I want you *with* me. That's a priority. Becoming a father starts with looking after you.'

Disconcerted by how strongly he stressed that reality, Bunny was relieved when the server entered with their meals. If they lived together, he would soon find out whether he wanted that kind of relationship or whether he preferred his loner lifestyle. If he walked away, she got hurt. If she had him and then lost him again, she would be hurt. It didn't seem to her that she had any true choice.

She sipped her water and then stuck out her left hand. 'You can put the ring on now.'

Sebastian vented a pained groan. 'All sentimental and soppy with bells on, right?'

'Well, you're the one who said he wanted to sign up for this,' she dared.

'Only because it's the only way I get you *and* the baby. I'm basic. I don't need frills.'

'I like frills...in the right place at the right time,' she countered as he slid the ring onto her wedding finger, where it glittered in the firelight. It fitted her very well, which she chose to take as a positive sign. 'It's an antique ring, isn't it?'

'It belonged to my Pagonis grandmother, Loukia.'

'She raised you, didn't she?' Bunny gathered while they ate.

'No, I was passed like a parcel nobody wanted to keep around the Pagonis tribe. Six months to a year with each set. Let's not talk about that now.'

Bunny had paled in dismay at the explanation but

she smiled and his brilliant dark gaze lingered on her with approval.

'We'll have to find somewhere to live. I assume you'll prefer to be within reach of your family?'

'If it were possible, yes,' she agreed.

'And your current employment isn't very suitable now that you're pregnant,' Sebastian pointed out. 'I don't want you out alone in some van at the back end of nowhere dealing with strangers.'

'The budget wouldn't stretch to an assistant. It's not what I imagined I'd be doing but you have to start at the bottom and work your way up the ladder.'

'Unless you're a Pagonis or attached to one,' Sebastian slotted in with amusement. Considering that he already had everything fully planned for their immediate future, he was relieved that he had very little left to do. 'I believe I can come up with a library for you to work in. *Thee mou*... I own an enormous amount of property. I suppose you want to go home to your family tonight.'

Bunny went pink and flashed her ring. 'Yes.'

'All I want is a bed and you and no interruptions.' That was a catchphrase for Sebastian, a mere soundbite. Everything was already organised, everything that would allow him to be the decent parent he himself had never had.

Bunny brushed her hair behind her ear and straightened her spine, a self-conscious smile playing with the corners of her mouth. 'Basic, well, you did warn me.'

His wide sensual lips settled into a smile, the last remnants of his tension evaporating. He had got more or less what he wanted, he conceded, and the bottom line was that he wanted *her*. Engaged, married, what was the difference? As long as she was with him, those frills she mentioned didn't matter. And possibly she was right. Maybe he *would* wake up in a few weeks and want his freedom back. He was as afraid of letting her down as he was of developing feelings for her. He wanted no part of the kind of dangerously possessive feelings his father had had for his mother.

'We'll wait until we've moved in together,' Sebastian decreed, on a roll now that he had achieved his goal. 'I want to take my time. When we get back together it won't be a temporary thing that reminds me of a one-night stand.'

'I want to take my time too,' Bunny sighed as they left the table and headed back outside. No hurried, stolen moments of passion for Sebastian, she thought ruefully. He wanted it *all*. He wanted perfection.

'You'll need to resign from your job,' he pointed out as he walked her back towards the car.

'Right now... I mean, *immediately*?' Bunny frowned in dismay and stopped dead in her tracks. 'I'll still have to work a month's notice. I won't let people down.'

'The longer you wait to leave, the longer it will be until we're living together.'

'You're the most shameless blackmailer!' Bunny

snapped furiously, ignoring the turned heads of his hovering security team as she stalked after him. 'But it doesn't mean I'll abandon my principles.'

'Principles have a cost,' Sebastian informed her without hesitation. 'I'm due in Germany to speak at an international conference next week and I also have a lengthy trip to Switzerland lined up.'

'That's perfect, then, isn't it?' Bunny dealt him a huge smile although she really wanted to slap him. He had expected her to fall into line because that was what people did for Sebastian Pagonis. He didn't accept her point of view because it didn't meet his wishes and expectations. 'While you're busy, I'll be busy too.'

'Not ideal though,' Sebastian incised.

'Moving home, resigning from my job, being with you. I wasn't expecting all of that. Six weeks ago, you didn't even hint that you wanted to see me again... It's all a lot to get my head around and you need to be less of a perfectionist.'

'I'm *not* a perfectionist,' he ground out through grated teeth.

'You so *are*. You laid every bonfire in a distinct pattern. You like everything in the correct order. You are never untidy or disorganised. I'm never going to live up to your standards, so you have to accept that now... On the other hand if you would admit to just wanting messy, ordinary, very human me, the sky's your limit!' she proclaimed in desperation, determined to get him out of the brooding mood that had engulfed him as the ramifications of her having refused his marriage proposal sank in.

It shouldn't be like that, not the same day he asked her to marry him and put an engagement ring on her finger, all of it so traditional and so *not* him. He had put on the suit, got down on one knee and it could only have been for *her* benefit and she had disappointed him, which made her feel hugely guilty and sad on his behalf. 'Sebastian...?'

'I'd better take you back to that van.'

Before he could start the car, she just snapped loose her seat belt and grabbed him, one set of fingers spearing into his dense black hair to bring his head down, the other yanking him towards her so that she could find his mouth. She kissed him and then he took over, ramming back his seat and hauling her onto his lap to savour her more passionately. And all the tension evaporated and birthed another kind of tension. It was as though a dam had burst and they were both so hungry for each other that neither one of them had the least control. His tongue delved deep and a growl sounded in his chest as his mouth tasted her delicate jawline and roamed down over the slender length of her neck to the slope of her shoulder. At the same time his big hands roamed over every part of her that he could reach. Bunny gasped and squirmed and tried frantically to get closer.

Sebastian expelled his breath on a hiss and lifted her to settle back into the passenger seat. 'I'll take you to the house we're going to be living in.'

'You already have a house picked?' Bunny demanded in amazement.

'You were right,' he conceded grudgingly. 'I plan *everything* and you gave me six weeks to do it in.'

'I didn't exactly give you six weeks...you kept your distance.'

'I won't be keeping my distance after tonight,' he warned her, laughing and leaning over her, long fingers sifting slowly through her thick silky hair. 'I'll pick you up after work and we'll tell your parents that we've got engaged and that you're moving out. But we won't see the house until tomorrow because I'd like you to see it in daylight first. Are we mentioning the baby?'

'No, not today.' Bunny's head was reeling at the knowledge that Sebastian was about to turn her life upside down. But they would be together. That was the bottom line, she reminded herself, and that was really all that mattered.

She was on a high throughout the afternoon. She put in her resignation but she saw no reason not to work her notice if Sebastian was going to be away on business. She could manage an hour commuting for the space of a month. Even though she would no longer have the use of her mother's car? There would probably be a train, she reasoned.

Sebastian followed her home. She had forgotten that it was a Friday night and the whole family would be there for dinner. Her mother gasped and cried when she saw the ring. Sebastian valiantly withstood being hugged for a solid five minutes and she could see that he was relieved when her father merely shook hands with him. He met her other brothers and their wives and girlfriends. He was much more relaxed and chatty than she would have expected and was predictably cornered by her youngest brother, Noah, who was the family tech whizz and he was eager to hear all about Sebastian's time at MIT.

Bunny ignored her usual wine and had a soft drink instead, reddening when she saw her brother, John, taking note of the fact. When she came out of the bathroom, John was waiting for her. 'So, you noticed,' she said with a rueful little smile.

'Of course, I did. Why didn't you tell me?'

'Because that was Sebastian's news to hear first and I didn't need to get advice on options from you because I already knew what I wanted,' she explained calmly. 'He asked me to marry him but I thought it was too soon for that. I think we should have some time together before we make that leap.'

John frowned in surprise. 'Considering that you've been pining for him since you got back, I'm amazed you didn't just say yes. You're being very sensible.'

'Not really. I'm moving in with him tomorrow. We'll see how that goes.'

'Why so pessimistic?'

'In his heart I'm not sure he's ready for a committed relationship.'

'Time will tell.'

Her parents asked Sebastian to stay and he thanked

them but insisted that he would see them in the morning when he collected Bunny.

'Nothing on earth would persuade me to enjoy our reunion sleeping next door to your parents,' he murmured wickedly in her ear when she saw him back to his car. 'You're quite noisy.'

'Am I?' she said, aghast and mortified.

'And I really like it,' he confided, lacing one hand into the fall of her hair and plundering her parted lips with passionate impatience. 'Your enthusiasm only matches my own.'

'Tristram?' Eyes wide, and having answered the bell while awaiting Sebastian, Bunny froze when she found her ex-boyfriend at the door.

He was a well-built young man of around six feet, with cropped blond hair and bright blue eyes. Once she had found him attractive, and his seemingly easy nature had charmed her. But now she fancied she could see the look of entitlement and arrogance in his expectant gaze because he assumed that she would be bowled over by his visit and delighted to see him again. Tristram never doubted the warmth of his welcome.

'I read about your dashing adventure in Asia and that you were now home. Aren't you going to invite me in?' Tristram asked.

'I'm sorry but there would be no point inviting you in because I'm about to go out,' Bunny advanced stiltedly, but she felt as if she was being rude and stepped outside to seem friendlier than she felt. 'I also don't see what we have to talk about.'

'You look amazing,' Tristram told her, noting the silky conditioned fall of her golden hair and her perfectly made-up face while the grape-coloured fitted skirt and silk shirt she wore enhanced her diminutive curves and small waist.

'Thanks.' Bunny would've liked to have said it was the first thing she threw on but in truth she had made an enormous effort on Sebastian's behalf. She had been waiting at the doors of the nearest local boutique at opening time and had blown everything in her bank account on a decent outfit and some make-up.

'You never made this much effort for me,' Tristram complained, his mouth taking on a sullen curve.

'But then, according to what I was told, you didn't make much effort for her,' Sebastian intoned from behind them both.

Bunny spun in concert with Tristram, who flushed angrily.

'Sebastian Pagonis... Tristram Elsworthy,' Bunny introduced stiffly.

Sebastian was seething, inflamed by the discovery of the ex on Bunny's doorstep. He dropped a territorial arm round her slight shoulders. 'We're running late,' he murmured apologetically.

Tristram backed off a step with a wide understanding smile. 'I won't keep you. I'll call another time, Bunny.'

'I'm afraid I won't be here, Tris. I'm moving,' she said pleasantly.

As her ex headed down the path to return to his car, Sebastian bit out in a raw undertone, 'You should've told him you were pregnant and engaged.'

'I wasn't about to give him private information like that!' Bunny objected.

But it was too late to be talking about what was private because Sebastian had given the game away. A gasp sounded in the hall of her parents' home. Bunny swivelled and saw her mother clamp her hand to her lips below her rounded and shocked eyes.

'Is it true?' the older woman asked.

And that was another hold-up as they went indoors to discuss that subject. Her mother shared the news that John's wife, Betsy, was expecting again, only she wasn't yet telling people, a meaningful restriction that seemed to have escaped her mother-in-law's understanding.

'Well, I must say that went down very well,' Sebastian remarked as they strolled out to the car, her luggage having been stowed while they talked. 'Your mother can't keep a secret.'

'I can't either...not very well or for very long,' Bunny confided guiltily. 'Why were you so angry at Tristram dropping in?'

Sebastian's sculpted jawline clenched. On the face of it, he didn't know why he'd been so angry. He simply didn't want her former boyfriend anywhere near Bunny. Even though the guy had backed off fast, Sebastian didn't like him showing up at Bunny's home and annoying her. That was normal. It didn't mean he was either fanatically possessive or obsessionally jealous, he assured himself. And it would be totally normal for him to check out Tristram Elsworthy and find out who he was.

'What did he want?'

'I haven't a clue. It's probably just one of those random things because he read about me being missing in a newspaper,' she framed. 'But you were so angry when you realised who he was, you went rigid.'

'I don't want him hanging around you,' Sebastian told her truthfully.

'Well, I'm not going to encourage him,' Bunny said cheerfully. 'I can't stand him. He's so fake and I see it now.'

But on one level, Sebastian was still brooding and annoyed that *he* had been annoyed about something so trivial. Even so, Tristram with the uber-short hair and the winning smile was her first love and women were said to be romantic and nostalgic about their first loves. Still troubled by the anger that had engulfed him, Sebastian was quiet.

'So why aren't you telling me anything about this house?' Bunny demanded as Sebastian steered the powerful car off the motorway and back into the countryside.

'It's a surprise. It's not modern but then you like history and old buildings, don't you?'

Her brow furrowed. 'How do you know that?'

'Don't you remember rabbiting on about how much you loved Hampton Court when we were on the island? About how you loved to tour old houses and imagine the people who had lived there? About how you believed that most contemporary furniture lacks character?'

Bunny burned with deep mortification. Certainly she had been guilty of rabbiting on a fair bit, which was why Sebastian was so very well acquainted with her likes and dislikes.

'The location of the house also had to be within reasonable reach of your family for you and close to London for me,' Sebastian added. 'I chose accordingly and I *nailed* it.'

'Did you indeed? What about your own preferences?'

'If a cave came with the usual mod cons I'd live in it. I picked this place based on *your* preferences because I don't really care about my domestic surroundings.'

'Did you buy this property specially?' she asked with a wince.

'*Thee mou*...the last thing we need to do in the Pagonis empire is buy property. I'd never seen the house until I visited it a few weeks ago but it *is* an inherited estate. It belonged to my grandfather's first wife, Rosalie. She was an orphaned only child when they married and she died in childbirth.'

'I didn't realise he'd been married more than once—'

'Neither did I until I grew up. My grandmother

must have been a little sensitive about being the *second* wife because she never mentioned her predecessor or as far as I know ever visited this place. It had tenants for decades and I had to throw an army of staff in to put it into order.'

A remarkable turreted and walled Tudor gateway greeted them at the foot of the country lane they were travelling. 'Where on earth are we visiting?' Bunny enquired, assuming this was a detour before the main event.

'Wait and see,' Sebastian urged.

Beyond the gates, long stretches of grass ran between ancient woodland trees and the lane branched to the right. Tall, elaborate chimneys pierced the skyline and then she saw the building. 'Where are we?'

'Our future home... Knightsmead Court.'

Bunny gaped at the ornate expanse of red brick and the lines of mullioned windows, utterly deprived of speech. 'It's glorious,' she whispered, pinching her forearm to be certain that she wasn't fantasising, because Sebastian was bringing her to her dream home. 'But it looks awfully big and not at all your style.'

'But very much yours,' Sebastian pointed out with assurance as he ran the Lamborghini to a halt on the gravel. 'Let's get out and explore.'

They stepped through a doorway above which a date in the sixteenth century was etched. An older woman welcomed them and Sebastian introduced them. Maybelle was the housekeeper. Bunny concentrated as much as she could on the conversation while sidling to the left to gaze into a log fire set in an opulently moulded chimneypiece. Warmth spilled out from the flames, lights flickering on polished oak furniture while flowers from an arrangement in the corner scented the air. To the rear a spectacular carved staircase wended up to the next floor with astonishing sculpted pineapples adorning the newel posts on the way. It was gorgeous while also being unexpectedly homely and warm.

'Let me show you to your new domain...' Sebastian urged, closing one hand over hers and walking her towards the back of the rambling house, his thumb caressing her slender wrist. 'After my grandfather's first wife died, the house was let but only after the most valuable furniture, paintings and books were removed and placed in safe storage. Everything has now been returned and here we have the library.' He flung open a heavy door into a large, very cluttered room, piled with specialist book storage boxes.

'Oh, my goodness!' Bunny exclaimed, scanning the two-tier room with its gallery and solid wooden staircase in one corner, not to mention the plethora of empty shelves waiting to be filled. 'But this room isn't from the Tudor era.'

'Of course not, and we can be grateful that the Victorians built a massive extension at the back of the house to house the library and various other things that were deemed necessities back in their day.'

'Grateful?' she queried in surprise.

'The extension was crumbling and threatening the

integrity of the original historic house but it couldn't be demolished because this is a listed building. The trade-off for restoring it at an incredible cost was being allowed to add bathrooms in the Victorian extension to make the house a little more habitable for our tenants.'

'This library is going to be a huge job,' she confided absently. 'And an absolute joy. Now I understand why you said that you had work for me.'

'As long as you understand that that work only starts when we return from Switzerland,' Sebastian extended lazily.

'We?' Bunny spun round and looked at him, automatically taking in the wickedly hot perfection of him sheathed in jeans and a black shirt that moulded every inch of his powerful torso and long, strong legs. Black diamond eyes glittered back at her in enquiring mode. 'But I'm not travelling to Switzerland with you.'

'Of course you are...and to Germany.'

Bunny blinked in bewilderment. 'No, I *can't*. I'll be working my notice for the next month.'

Sebastian stilled, lean, darkly handsome features tightening. 'Even after I told you how I felt about that?'

'Just a few weeks and then they'll have someone who will take over when I leave. That way the readers won't be left without the service and disappointed,' she reasoned awkwardly, but her conviction that she was doing what was right remained unshaken.

'What about *me* being disappointed?' Sebastian breathed in a bitter undertone. 'Where do I come into this decision?'

Bunny's heart sank on the realisation that they had hit a sticking point, one of those concealed tripwires or triggers that set couples at odds when they didn't know each other well enough to know what the other party wanted. And the awful truth was that Sebastian hadn't come into her decision at all because he hadn't told her that he wanted her with him when he went abroad.

CHAPTER NINE

'Well, you didn't really come into the decision because it's my life and my reputation at stake, not yours,' Bunny proffered tightly. 'And it's only for a month, Sebastian! The way you're reacting, you'd think I'd decided to work miles away for the next year at least. I had absolutely no idea that you were expecting me to travel with you, *be* with you when you're working. You didn't share that wish with me.'

'I didn't,' Sebastian conceded between teeth that sounded gritted.

He had had everything planned but plans fell through, especially with Bunny in the driving seat. She was bone-deep stubborn. She had said no to marriage, which had thrown him onto the defensive. He had dealt with that setback, however, had accepted that he was pretty much on probation as a would-be husband. As a result, he had worked to make everything else perfect for her. However, the simply wanting her with him, wanting her within reach, had fallen apart as a goal as well. And he couldn't believe it because he had made so much effort on her behalf.

For the very first time he was really *trying* with a woman, but she hadn't budged an inch from her previous stance. *Was* he being unreasonable? He was willing to admit that he was demanding, but nothing had ever been as important to him as she was.

'I'm sorry that I've disappointed you,' Bunny murmured unhappily in the long tense silence. 'I assumed that you'd be busy working so it wouldn't matter to you if I was working as well.'

'You'll have to have a bodyguard with you when you're out doing those library stops,' Sebastian told her grimly. 'I don't want you alone in quiet places, at risk from any passing pervert or psychopath.'

Bunny rolled her eyes and Sebastian dealt her a slashing glance of reproof. 'These things happen and I won't have it happen to you…or our baby.'

Discomfiture writhed through Bunny as it occurred to her that such a devastating, unforeseen incident had happened to him as a child. 'I wanted to work my notice rather than walk out because who knows what's in the future? I don't want a big black mark on my CV if I were to seek work in the library sector again.'

'Do I really deserve another pessimistic forecast from your corner? Even if we part unmarried, I will make a very generous settlement on you and our child. In all likelihood you will never work for a living again…unless you choose to do so.'

At that information, which merely increased her insecurity about their future as a couple, Bunny hovered uneasily, trying to read his shuttered expression and failing. 'What would I have done with myself anyway while you were working on your business trips? Did you think of that?'

'No,' Sebastian admitted in a roughened undertone. 'I simply wanted you *with* me.'

'And you've got me now for the whole weekend,' Bunny reminded him.

'Aren't I fortunate that you don't work on Saturdays?' he sniped.

At his most basic, he just wanted her with him and that was a compliment, an expression of need and want he would never make more openly. Her heart clenched, sudden tears striking the backs of her eyes, and she cursed those pregnancy hormones turning her into a dripping tap.

'I would've preferred to be with you too,' she muttered, moving closer in slow steps. 'Nothing would have made me happier, but I won't let people down unless I have no other choice. I won't be selfish like that.'

She closed her arms round his still figure, drinking in the rich scent of him like the addict she was. Man and musk, a hint of cologne, and that incredible underlying familiar scent that washed over her in the most enervating, satisfying way. Her hands ran up over his strong back, feeling his slight movements in the ripple of his muscles, registering the instinctive surge of her own response: the tight nipples, the racing heartbeat, the heated ache between her legs, the physical craving that never stopped.

'*Thee mou...* I want you,' he groaned rough and low into the springy depths of her hair. 'I wanted you every night, every morning...'

'So, do something about it,' she whispered in helpless encouragement.

He said nothing. He simply lifted her up into his arms like a caveman and ravished her mouth with raw, demanding hunger. Her fingernails raked and bit into his broad shoulders as she steadied herself as the same urgency rocketed through her like a heat-seeking missile. He carried her out of the library and started up the stairs, talking the whole time.

'I had this fantasy about you last night while you were being so correct and well behaved in front of your family,' he confided. 'You were wearing a corset and black stockings, usually not my thing but stuff like that would suit you...must buy you some.'

'You're much more experienced than me,' she sighed. 'I've never done the lingerie parade for a guy.'

'I'd enjoy it...occasionally. You can be whoever you want to be with me. There are no restrictions. '

'You surprise me. You're such a bossy-boots,' she told him.

'You surprised me the first night. You weren't too shy to go after what you wanted...and you wanted me. It made me feel *amazing*,' he admitted thickly. 'It wasn't the money or the Pagonis name, it was only me as I am and that *did* it for me.'

'Did it really?' she teased as he elbowed his passage into a wainscoted room where the autumn gloom was brightened by lamps with a fire crackling some place out of view. He leant her back against the door and began to inch up her skirt.

'It's too tight for that,' she warned him. 'There's a zip.'

'Should've noticed that,' he grumbled, running down the zip until the fitted skirt puddled at her feet and he lifted her out of it. It took about thirty seconds for the shirt to fall and then he was tracing the prominent buds of her nipples, fingertips light over the swollen buds visible through the lace of her bra. He tugged down the straps on her shoulders, eased the cups down and bent his dark head. Her head threw back against the door as a moan exploded from her lungs, his tongue lashing the sensitive peaks, need tugging at her feminine core with velvet claws.

Sebastian dropped to his knees, long fingers skimming down the panties she wore, swiping them out of his way. And then he found her with his mouth where she was swollen and damp and throbbing. As he devoured her, she gasped, head falling back again, pleasure seizing her in a fierce grip for long timeless moments until the ultimate high detonated throughout her entire body and she cried out in climax. As her legs buckled, his big hands closed over her hips and he lifted her to lower her down onto a soft, comfortable bed. He detached her bra, cast it aside, smoothed both of his hands up to cup the pouting flesh. His fingers found the sensitised buds, strummed and teased until her back was arching.

Sensation sizzled through Bunny in spasms of tormenting bliss, her body building up, the intense craving tightening again like a knot inside her, making her buck and squirm in delight. She had missed him, she had really, really missed him, not only the sex but the intimacy of being with him, waking up beside him in the morning, falling asleep in his arms. As she writhed, her head tossing on the pillow, she was moaning, gasping his name like a mantra, and then the whole intensity of the experience sent her flying up into the stars in the hold of another breathtaking climax.

'Still with me?' Sebastian purred with his irreverent grin, leaning down over her to kiss her breathless.

'You've still got all your clothes on!' she complained.

His eyes darkened. 'Not for long,' he assured her as he began to strip.

And she watched while the shirt was peeled off, the shoes kicked aside, the jeans tossed aside. It was one of her favourite activities: enjoying the sight of Sebastian's beautiful body naked. Her heart raced a little faster, her inner muscles clenched in anticipation. He came down to her, all trace of his earlier dissatisfaction gone.

'Am I forgiven yet?'

Sebastian frowned. 'You're here now. Only fools sweat the small stuff.'

Bunny threaded her fingers through his tousled long black hair and traced his wide sensual mouth with her fingertips. 'I'm sorry I spoiled the plans you had made but will you please stop talking about the money you intend to give me if we break up?'

'If you faithfully promise to say nothing more about any future you might have that does not include me,' he bargained.

Bunny nodded and smiled at that request, and he tipped her back, rising over her with easy strength, sliding into her hot, tight channel with urgent intensity and then groaning with uninhibited pleasure. 'What a relief it is to no longer have to worry about our lack of birth control.'

Bunny laughed, taking herself by surprise. 'Yes, you weren't very good at the self-denial bit.'

He shifted his lithe hips, sending fresh little tendrils of desire travelling through her, and she moaned, unashamed to show her pleasure. 'Am I allowed to admit that I enjoyed failing?' he confessed.

He had stoked her hunger again. As he began to move more forcefully, she gave herself up to that raw surge of passion again. In the midst of it, he momentarily frustrated her by pausing to put her into another position and then, when that change enhanced her enjoyment, she was thrilled by the wild, exhilarating ride that followed. Her heart thundered, heat and perspiration flushing her skin, excitement gathering and surging through her veins until a supernova explosion of pleasure shattered the last of her control and she slumped, absolutely exhausted.

'That was spectacular,' Sebastian purred in satiated conclusion, releasing her from his weight and gathering her close.

Her drowsy eyelashes fluttered and she snuggled back into him. 'I love you,' she mumbled, and then her eyes opened very wide in dismay and she mentally kicked herself for letting relaxation control her.

'No, you don't,' Sebastian contradicted with succinct bite. 'It's habit, familiarity, a certain amount of affection but it's *not* love. Nobody has ever loved me.'

Bewildered, disconcerted and suddenly propelled into a new state of alertness, Bunny blinked. 'Your mother...surely?'

'My most common memory of my mother is of her waving as she went out. She was a jet-setter with a giddy social life. I remember my first nanny better than her.'

'Your grandmother, then.'

'Only when I reminded her of the late son she couldn't mention and not so as you would notice while I was growing up without my parents. I stayed with her twice a year, at Christmas and in the summer.'

'Why was that?' she asked with a pained frown.

'Everyone told her she had messed up my father by spoiling him rotten and she felt very guilty and blamed herself for what my father did. It made her take a hands-off approach with me.'

'Was she right to feel guilty?'

'I don't know,' Sebastian mused. 'My grandfather died, leaving her a single parent of five young children. She also had a huge property empire to run. I doubt that a man would be judged so harshly for his parenting flaws.'

'But you still think that basically you're...what? Unlovable?' she pressed.

'No. I think people's feelings change on the turn of a dime.'

'I have parents and grandparents whose long marriages would disprove that. I think you have to work and compromise to sustain a long relationship, but I do think it's possible,' she countered. 'And don't tell me what I feel. That's my business. Only I know how I feel but I'll keep it to myself in future. If you're still around when I'm seventy-five, I'll be throwing this conversation in your face daily.'

An involuntary smile of relief softened the tense line of Sebastian's lean dark features as her last comment lessened the tension. 'I can imagine that.'

Of course, she didn't love him, he reasoned. Why would she? Right now, she was on a high of great sex, affection and happiness because they were together and she liked the house. And possibly there was even a pregnancy happy hormone? *Was* there? But he had to be honest with her about where he stood and keep it real between them. Better that she understood him from the start than began nourishing hopes he couldn't fulfil. At the same time, he was wondering if she truly believed she loved him and, if she did believe it, what did it *feel* like? And wasn't it weird in such circumstances to wonder what falling in love felt like?

Bunny reckoned that she would never tell him she loved him again. He didn't want her love because he flat out didn't believe in it. There wasn't much that she could do about that. An ache stirred in the region of her heart nonetheless because she, of course, wanted him to love her back. But did love matter if he still wanted her, needed her and treated her well? Only what would keep him with her in a crisis? Their child, whom he believed he *would* love? That suspicion made her heart sink because naturally she needed to be loved for herself and not only for the little passenger she currently carried.

There was no sleeping for her after that stirring exchange. He showed her into a massive contemporary bathroom and through a connecting door into a dressing room already packed with garments. 'You needed clothes. I didn't order maternity stuff because I had no idea what you would like. But there should be enough in the new wardrobe to cover most social engagements.'

Taken aback by yet another giant demonstration of Sebastian's instinctive generosity, Bunny winced. 'Sebastian...er, I don't have social engagements.'

'Your first is only a week away. Next Saturday, we're having a party here for you to meet my friends. Dress formal. There should be a selection of evening gowns in the closets. The week after we're flying to Greece for you to meet my family and won't that be fun?'

'Meaning?'

'Half of them are trying to sue me through the courts at the minute for a share of my grandmother's wealth.'

'Your family's *doing* that to you?'

'Money talks louder than blood in the Pagonis tribe,' he warned her. 'Even better, my uncles and cousins all work for me now.'

Bunny knew sarcasm when she heard it now and she recognised his bitterness too. She had serious questions to ask about his childhood but decided to leave them until later. 'So when do I get the full tour of the house?' she asked instead.

'As soon as you're dressed and we've had lunch.' His dazzling smile engulfed her and she was aware that his extra warmth stemmed from her having restrained her uncomfortable curiosity.

She hastened into the shower to freshen up while wondering with a pleasant sense of anticipation about what lay within those closets. She had never had the money to buy fancy clothes but she loved to dress up. It would be mortifying though to embarrass Sebastian by looking shabby and she was relieved that he had taken care of the problem.

Forty minutes later, she wore light wool trousers, a rather slinky blue top and a cashmere cardigan teamed with soft leather boots. Knightsmead Court had all the drawbacks of a historic listed property. Away from the fireplaces and the background heating provided by a system installed in the twenties, it could be chilly. Pausing only to admire the magnificent four-poster bed, which was enormous and unbelievably comfortable and hung with gorgeous brocade drapes, she smiled at Sebastian.

'How did you know I love four-poster beds?'

'An extensive amount of online snooping. Your footprint is very heavy on four-poster beds. This one is brand new and made to order. I'm too big for an antique bed and I expect a decent mattress,' he told her.

Bunny blinked and went pink at the thought of him going to that much trouble to establish her likes and dislikes. Did it bother her that he admitted to snooping? Not particularly because she had nothing to hide from him. It said much more about him, she reckoned, that he had put her preferences above his own. Pleased, she allowed him to lead her on a tour. There was so much for her to admire. The airy long gallery where the ladies had once taken their exercise in adverse weather, the carved chimneypieces and wainscoted walls, the great hall with its minstrels' gallery and walls hung with shields, medieval weapons and faded flags.

'The perfect backdrop for a party...or a wedding reception,' Sebastian remarked. 'That is assuming we don't go for a guest list of thousands.'

'We're not talking weddings yet,' she reminded

him. 'But I would only have friends and family. I should imagine your list would have hundreds of possibilities, business and social.'

'My wedding wouldn't be a business event,' he murmured, opening a door at the end of the hall to usher her into a more reasonably sized dining room where there were a polished table, fine bone china and candelabra, and yet another fire glowed in a giant grate.

'Who's keeping all these fires going?' she exclaimed in wonderment.

'We have a large staff here.'

'Is there an estate with the house?'

'No, there's a home farm and woods and sufficient land to preserve privacy but the majority of the original estate was sold off long before my grandfather met his first wife.'

'Tragic her dying in childbirth and the baby dying as well,' she sighed.

'It's not going to happen with you. You will have every medical exam available and, by the way,' Sebastian continued, 'I organised an appointment for you on Monday to see an obstetrician for the usual checks. I'll go with you before I leave for Germany.'

'I was going to get around to it eventually, but then I don't really need to think for myself any more with you so happy to do *all* my thinking for me,' she said drily.

'Touché,' he responded without heat. 'I always think ahead. Occasionally it irritates people.'

Their lunch arrived, brought in by an elderly man with a stately manner.

'This is Parker, Bunny. Our butler, who has always worked here and knows everything there is to know about this house,' Sebastian advanced.

'Madam...sir.' Parker executed a slight bow. 'I am happy to still be here.'

'I'm glad you kept him on,' Bunny whispered when he had left them alone again. 'But he must be at least—'

'Seventy-eight, but he doesn't want to retire. He's Maybelle's father,' Sebastian supplied as she shed her cardigan in the heat flowing from the fire. 'And, in what he terms the twilight of his life, presiding over a large staff with an enhanced salary and a large household budget suits him very well.'

Bunny laughed and then her heart-shaped face turned serious. 'It's time you told me about what happened to you after your parents passed away...'

Sebastian flinched. 'The Pagonis family were devastated by the scandal and the shame of what my father did. As the survivor, I was a huge embarrassment and a disappointment. They put out a story that my father had mental health issues, which was untrue. They refused to admit his addiction. They made me see a psychiatrist every week for years and sent me to boarding school in England where I could be forgotten about.' Sebastian toasted her with his wine glass and lounged back in his seat, his lean, darkly handsome features taut. 'Vacation times? They sent me off to wilderness survival camps and places for troubled adolescents because nobody wanted me around.'

'But why was it like that?' she demanded with a frown.

'If I'd died that night, the family wealth would have gone to my four uncles, who had all fiercely resented my father. My grandfather tied everything up in a trust which leaves *everything* to the firstborn son and Loukia didn't challenge her husband's trust arrangements while she was alive. The family thought they would come into her property empire but it had originally been my grandfather's, so it also came to me. I'm already rich beyond avarice. Her will was the last straw, which is why they're dragging me through the courts...and destined to lose. The trust as it currently stands is virtually unbreakable.'

'So what do you plan to do?'

'In the interests of fairness, offer them a decent settlement, continue to employ them and revise that trust for my child's sake and ensure that a daughter will not be discounted. I'm determined to prevent the bitterness revisiting the next generation if we have more than one child,' he proffered calmly.

Bunny nodded thoughtfully. 'That's sensible.'

But she wasn't thinking about the money, she was thinking about a little boy sent abroad for his education because he was an uber-wealthy child and resented for it by those who might instead have shown him love and understanding. And she understood so much more about Sebastian in that moment. He had been forced to be a loner, forced into his general attitude of distrust with the rest of the world because his family had failed him and if family didn't step up to help and care, why would you expect anyone else to do so? He didn't believe in love because he hadn't had love but perhaps that outlook could be softened by time. And was she prepared to give him that time? The longer she stayed with him, the harder it would be to leave.

And Sebastian had made it that way quite deliberately whether he saw that or not. He had put together her dream house and her dream library. He would give her everything from a four-poster bed to a designer wardrobe but he wouldn't give her love. Sebastian, she realised without surprise, was clever enough to also be intensely manipulative. He made her feel safe but was that safety an illusion?

CHAPTER TEN

Bunny descended the Tudor staircase sheathed in a red designer halter-neck dress that skimmed forgivingly over the slight new curve of her tummy.

It had been a busy week, starting with her first appointment with the obstetrician, a lovely woman in her thirties who had once worked with Sebastian. The blood test had revealed that their unborn child was a boy. And with that groundbreaking news, she had started working her notice at the library, only that hadn't lasted long because the runner-up for her job had proved to be still available and eager to start as soon as possible. Naturally she had stepped down early to facilitate a transfer that would suit everyone better. Going to work complete with a security team had entailed constant explanations, which had quickly become embarrassing.

'Don't blame Sebastian for having you guarded like the Crown Jewels,' her mother had enthused when Bunny had dared to vent her irritation. 'He lost everything when he lost his parents. Naturally he's terrified of it happening again.'

As that angle had not occurred to her, she had kept her irritation to herself and had accepted her carload of security personnel, who loved it when she visited her parents, where they got treated to cake and coffee.

Sebastian had been in Germany for three days and when he had reappeared had draped a fabulous diamond pendant round her neck and matched it with a pair of stunning earrings. Herding her into their capacious shower clad only in diamonds, he had made passionate love to her and had complained bitterly about how much he had missed her. After only three days apart, she had believed that that was quite promising in terms of attachment. She was starting to think that with Sebastian she needed to pay less heed to what he said and more heed to his actions.

Sebastian strolled out of the great hall, from which the chink of glasses and a low hum of conversation emanated, to greet her. He looked shockingly hot in a tailored black dinner jacket and narrow trousers, having explained that he would dress up because his friends enjoyed 'that sort of thing'. Even if he didn't, he wore that polished sophisticated apparel well. Mentally she kicked herself for not recalling the kind of privileged world that Sebastian had grown up in when there must've been many occasions when he had had to wear such clothing simply to fit in.

She walked into a crowded room filled with gowned women sparkling with precious jewellery and well-groomed men. Her nerves were on high.

'This is Bunny, my fiancée,' Sebastian announced with quiet satisfaction, one hand clasped to her back.

And a literal squeal erupted from a small, bubbly brunette, who sped forward to look at the beautiful ring on Bunny's finger and give Sebastian a warm hug. There was a welter of conjecture. Sebastian admitted freely to having been shipwrecked and stranded with her, being much more open than she was accustomed to him being, and it had the effect of relaxing her. These were people he trusted.

'I'm Zoe, Andreas's wife,' the petite brunette proffered. 'I had to come and meet you. It's a long way to come for a party but we've known Sebastian for so many years that I had to meet the woman who finally cracked his ice heart.'

Bunny recalled the friendly Andreas from their rescue but he had vanished again soon afterwards, and she went pink and muttered ruefully, 'Oh, I hope there was no cracking of hearts, unless it was mine, and mine is certainly not ice.'

'No, you misunderstand,' Zoe assured her. 'I know you are a hundred per cent special because I first met Sebastian when he was seventeen and he has never introduced a woman to us, not *once* in all this time. There've been women—I have no doubt—offstage, as it were, but never one who was a companion, a partner like you. I thought he would be single until the day he died.'

'My word, you're making me feel good,' Bunny said quietly, but, much as she longed to stay with someone who knew Sebastian that well, there were others waiting to meet her and she knew her manners. 'Hopefully see you later?'

'You can bet on it,' Zoe told her warmly.

'Enjoying yourself?' Sebastian asked her later as he drew her out onto the temporary dance floor laid out at the foot of the great hall.

'Yes. You have some lovely friends, but I was surprised so many were medics,' she confided.

'You get to know people really well when you train and work in medicine. Genuine people, who don't give a damn about my wealth or my dodgy background.'

'It's not dodgy. For goodness' sake, that tragedy wasn't *your* fault!' she exclaimed in annoyance on his behalf.

Sebastian groaned above her head and steered her into a proper dance but she had never learned how to do that and she tripped over his feet several times before surrendering and retiring to the sidelines with a giggle. 'You'll have to give me lessons if you want the fancy stuff,' she warned him.

'I've got family jewellery for you to wear in Greece next week,' he told her.

'Your grandmother's?'

'Yes, the pieces she had to pass down. Her personal collection went to her surviving sons, aside from the engagement ring you're wearing, which she left to me. And I thought that was a bad joke because I never planned to marry,' he murmured soft and low, and they stopped dancing altogether as he lifted his head to stare down at her. 'And then, only a few weeks later, I met *you*...'

Bunny grinned up at him. 'You see, being a loner is not as much fun as you used to think!'

Sebastian rested his hands on her slight shoulders and looked down at her lovely smiling face with smouldering dark eyes. He said something in Greek and then he stretched down to steal a hungry kiss and a flame ignited between her thighs, making her throb, and she pressed her legs together tightly to contain that surge of hunger.

As she walked out to the cloakroom a few minutes later Zoe appeared by her side. 'He's besotted with you,' the Greek woman said cheerfully. 'Have you set a wedding date yet?'

'No, not yet. Sebastian doesn't do love.'

'Maybe not but that's what's written all over his face every time he looks at you, so Eros must not have been listening when he put you two together. I believe in fate.'

Bunny smiled. 'When there's a wedding date—' she chose her answer with care '—you'll be the first to know.'

A week later they were in Greece but with far less relaxing company. Bunny wore an evening gown that would have been fit for a red-carpet appearance. Mostly black, it shone with iridescent crystals that reflected the light in a soft rainbow of colour.

At her throat she wore the magnificent Pagonis emerald necklace and the matching drops in her ears and with Sebastian's hand splayed possessively at her spine she walked like a queen, determined not to be 'less' in the presence of the relatives who had treated their nephew so poorly as a child and not much better since.

Everyone was icily polite. They sat down to dine in a giant town house in Athens at a table that seated forty guests. Every eye in the room rested on their every move and she could see that her existence, the underwritten knowledge that Sebastian would marry and presumably have a child someday, was not good news on their terms. But she ignored it, stayed courteous, agonised over what Sebastian must have undergone as a kid in so chilly an atmosphere, and inwardly cursed them all to hell for what they had put him through out of greed and resentment of his privileged position as firstborn of his generation.

When the evening was done, she heaved a huge sigh of relief and accompanied Sebastian upstairs to their bedroom. 'Gosh, that was exhausting...what a horrible bunch of folk! Sorry, I shouldn't say that about family members but when I think of how lucky I've been with mine and how unlucky you've been, it just makes me so *mad*,' she framed furiously.

'You don't need to be mad. The time when it could hurt to be treated that way is far behind me and, if it helps, we only have to see them a couple of times a year,' he assured her wryly. 'I'm head of the family now, like it or not, and we can always hope that the younger generation will be more accepting.'

'Accepting of what?' Bunny exclaimed. 'The fact that you were born rich? That you employ them? That you're a huge success in business? There is nothing unacceptable about you, Sebastian. They are the ones with the problem, *not* you!'

In the act of wrenching off his bow tie, shedding the dinner jacket, Sebastian had paused, and slowly, as she spoke, a smile began to grow at the corners of his handsome mouth, his lean, strong face starting to lose the tension that the dinner party had roused in him.

He began to unhook her elaborate gown, smoothing her soft skin as he exposed more of it, sending a shiver of awareness through her small frame. 'I like when you defend me with such vehemence. You're so loyal. I appreciate that, having someone on *my* side for a change.'

Bunny turned round in the circle of his arms and stretched up on tiptoe to try and kiss him but it was virtually impossible and, with a chuckle, he lifted her up to him. 'Want something, short stuff?'

'I'm not short. I am average. You're the one topping the excessive scale,' she teased back.

'Is that so?' Her dress, which had left her shoulders bare, fluttered in a cloud of costly fabric to the floor, leaving her clad only in her lingerie. 'I like this view.'

'Put me down,' she urged.

He settled her down on the edge of the bed and studied her closely. 'I want us to set a wedding date. I'm tired of being asked...*when*? I'd also like to be married before the baby's born.'

Colour flushed her cheeks and she threaded a harried hand through the now tousled strands of her long hair, half turning her head away from his glittering dark scrutiny. 'I—'

'And if your answer is still no, I want to know why. We've been together almost a month. You seem happy—'

'I *am* happy!' Bunny broke in, thinking that she had never been happier in her life before. 'But I still think it's too soon.'

'It's not too soon for me,' Sebastian countered with a roughened edge to his dark, deep drawl. 'Why would it still be too soon for you?'

Loathing being put on the spot in such a way, Bunny got off the bed and said lamely, 'It just is!' As if that were an explanation, when really it was the only explanation she had that she was willing to offer.

She vanished into the en suite to take off her make-up and freshen up. The door behind her opened, framing Sebastian. Faint colour burned along the exotic line of his high cheekbones and his narrowed dark golden eyes were brilliant and focused hard on her. 'Explain,' he told her. 'You didn't foresee this problem when you suggested that we get engaged instead of married, did you?'

'No,' she conceded, squirming at that mistake on her part. 'And that was very shortsighted of me. I just didn't want to risk your idea of being with me changing. I wanted you to have more time.'

Sebastian flung his handsome head back in a sudden movement. 'How much *more* time?' he demanded rawly. 'I feel like I'm on trial here, Bunny. I asked you to marry me, which was *huge* for me.'

'I know... I know,' she began, frantically struggling to think of what to say to satisfy him.

'I'm fully committed to you. It is not unreasonable to ask you for a date,' he ground out.

Anger was poisoning the air, gathering round her like a dark cloud. There was a very slight shake in his dark deep voice. She knew that he was furious with her, striving to control his temper. Sebastian, who almost never lost control of his emotions. She felt like the worst person in the world for making him feel so frustrated with her. She felt as though she had let him down. And then it was as though all the air, toxic or otherwise, had been sucked away from her because Sebastian just turned on his heel and walked away.

'Where are you going?' she gasped, trailing after him.

'I can't stay with you tonight,' Sebastian said gruffly without turning his head as he opened the bedroom door. 'I'm out of patience. It seems like I want much more than you're prepared to give me and I'm banging my head up against a brick wall.'

The door thudded on his departure, and, in a daze, she got ready for bed. Why couldn't she simply agree to marry him? Was it because of Tristram telling her that he wanted her to marry him even though there had been no ring or even a mention of meeting his family? He had strung her along that way for months on end, insisting he cared for her when patently he didn't.

Had she really withheld her consent to marriage because Sebastian couldn't offer her love? After all, he had offered her so many other important things. Like a beautiful home at Knightsmead Court, furnished even to her preferences. He had been unashamedly emotional when he'd viewed their little blip on the ultrasound screen. He looked after her in every possible way. He was everything she wanted, everything she loved. Was she the one with the problem, rather than him? And why was that?

She lay sleepless all night working it out. She didn't feel good enough for Sebastian Pagonis and that basic truth hit her hard. She was an ordinary girl without a pedigreed background, so why would he want her? After all, Tristram hadn't really wanted her when it came down to brass tacks. At least, he hadn't wanted her *enough*. Had she been trying to ensure that Sebastian did want her enough to stay with her for good? But how could anyone prove that in advance?

All she had done was make Sebastian feel as if *he* weren't good enough. He felt as though he were on trial. She shivered at that idea, that she could have subjected him to feeling like that. She was cold in the early morning light filtering through the windows because she hadn't closed the curtains, cold inside and out because Sebastian wasn't with her, lighting up her world the way he usually did. And hadn't she taken that for granted?

That he would keep on trying? Keep on trying to prove himself?

Her heart sank. Love was supposed to be kind and caring and generous but what had she given him? Reaching a sudden decision, Bunny sprang out of bed, weary and heavy-eyed but determined to set that date for Sebastian and apologise for all the insecurities that had subconsciously trapped her. She pulled on a robe and went to look for him.

In an unfamiliar house, that wasn't an easy task. She checked several empty bedrooms, marvelling that such a large property was maintained simply for the couple of annual family get-togethers Sebastian tolerated for the sake of courtesy. If he ever forgave her for infuriating him to such an extent, she would suggest that he found somewhere else for such meetings because he had admitted that he didn't use the Athens house on any other occasion. Unhappily, no bedroom contained him. She returned to her room and showered and dressed, seriously worried that she had no idea where he had gone.

It was one of her bodyguards who let her into that secret by asking her when she wished to head to the airport for their return flight to the UK. 'What does Sebastian want?'

He frowned in bewilderment. 'Mr Pagonis flew to Switzerland at six this morning...'

And belatedly she recalled him mentioning something about that change of flight plan while she had been dressing for that awful dinner the night before. Gloom set in then, over her solitary breakfast. She tried to phone him. The call, unusually, wasn't answered. Convinced he still wasn't speaking to her, she desisted from sending a flood of texts, although it was a challenge when she knew that it would be a week before she saw him again.

She travelled back to Knightsmead, feeling as though she were carting around her own very personal little black cloud. She had been selfish, unreasonable and shortsighted and she wasn't accustomed to seeing such traits in herself, so *that* knowledge couldn't lift her spirits.

She spent a lot of her time with her family that week, until suspicious eyes began to turn in her direction and pretending that everything was fine became too much of a strain. For the first time in her pregnancy, she felt nauseous and reckoned it was simply nerves and a lost appetite. Her brother John called in when she was working in the library.

'Don't be trying to lift that,' he warned her when he found her crouched over a book box.

'No, don't worry, I'm just digging through it. There are books that need restoration and I'm setting them aside first...new bindings, torn pages. Some of them are very old and need special care,' she explained.

'Parker said he'd bring us tea and snacks in here. I've only got an hour before my next appointment. Do you mind if I leave you being industrious and go and have a snoop round your fabulous home for myself?' her brother enquired with amusement.

'Not at all. Go ahead,' she encouraged, because, unlike the rest of her family, John had been too busy to come for the original tour she had offered them. Like her, he was into history and would enjoy browsing alone more.

She rose on her socked feet off the rug. Sebastian had warned her that she was to lift nothing as well. Well, so much for his caring side, she thought painfully, when his polite phone calls had done nothing to mend the breach between them. Did he sulk? This was where you discovered that Mr Perfect wasn't, after all, Mr Perfect, she reflected heavily. But then she hadn't tackled the controversial subject of when they might marry on the phone either, she acknowledged wearily.

She lifted the heavy family bible she wanted to place on the upper gallery table where—according to Parker—it had always sat. Being almost as old as the library, Parker was a font of knowledge about such matters.

She carted the giant book with care in her gloved hands and mounted the wooden staircase. Reaching the gallery, she settled the old family bible back in its former resting place. Flushed with success, she started down the stairs again at speed and, whether it was the socks on her feet or the gloves she wore for handling ancient books, she slid like a sledder at the top of a mountain on a big run. With a sharp cry of alarm, she tried to right her balance, but it was too late. She went bumpety, bumpety bump down the stairs and landed awkwardly with a twisted ankle.

Parker burst in with all the urgency of an ambulance and knelt down by her side, wringing his worn hands in horror and dismay. 'Miss Woods… Miss Woods, what do I do?'

'I'll handle this…' John appeared, frowning down at her. 'You went up those stairs without shoes on, didn't you? And those stupid slippery gloves? Do you have a death wish?' he asked quietly as Parker sped from the room, thoroughly unsettled by her accident.

Bunny didn't rise to the bait, because of course John the ever practical was right. 'I've hurt my ankle, probably going to have a few bruises on my bottom as well,' she groaned as he helped her up and into the nearest armchair.

She withstood a lecture about being more careful now that she was pregnant and hung her head, misery choking her. Just then she didn't care about anything and she knew she had not hurt her baby, only her ankle and her back. She deserved the bruises for being so careless, she thought miserably as her brother bandaged her ankle for her, offered to take her to the hospital if she was apprehensive and looked relieved at her refusal.

Parker brought in the tea with an air of satisfaction. 'Mr Pagonis is on his way home,' he announced.

'But he's not supposed to be back for another couple of days!' Bunny gasped in surprise, underlaid with a strong sense of relief. The sooner she saw him, the sooner she could cross the chasm of the separation she had caused. And she glanced down at herself, noting her ancient comfy jeans, her shapeless sweater, the kind of clothes she put on when she was in a down mood. That wasn't how she wanted to greet Sebastian. Having shared a cup of tea with her brother before he rushed off, she hobbled awkwardly upstairs to shower and change.

Restricted as she was, everything took longer than usual and it hurt hovering on one leg to dry her hair and put on some make-up. The results, however, far outweighed the discomfort. She limped into the dressing room for fresh undies, donning pretty lace pastels in a soft green before rifling in the closet for a dress. It was a little chilly for a dress but she shouldn't be thinking of such practicalities, she warned herself, tugging the stretchy dark green designer garment over her head and shimmying her hips while wondering uncertainly whether going barefoot would be sexier than wearing only one shoe.

Sebastian, as he surged upstairs like a man on a mission, however, had far more pressing concerns. Parker had phoned him while he was in a meeting in

Geneva and his brain had gone pretty blank during that brief call, only parts of it staying with him. An accident...a fall...her brother, the doctor, with her. It had traumatised him: the prospect of losing Bunny and the baby, the very idea of them being ripped from his world. Slowly, on the flight back home, he had pulled himself together and another phone conversation with John had reassured him that no great harm had been done, only to Parker, who had panicked.

They were okay, they were okay, Sebastian kept reminding himself, but nothing could dim his urgent need to see Bunny in the flesh. He stopped dead in surprise when he saw her balancing on one leg by gripping one of the posts of the bed, striving to get her foot into one high heel.

'What are you doing?' Sebastian demanded, crossing the room so fast that he left her breathless and lifting her off her feet to lay her down on the bed. 'John said you had to rest it and with the amount of bandaging he's put on your foot, you couldn't get it into a shoe.'

'You're so practical,' Bunny muttered in shaken complaint because popular belief would have suggested that Sebastian should have paused to note how groomed she was looking and to express his appreciation. Unhappily, Sebastian was more interested in probing her ankle and her foot, undoing the bandage, putting it on more tightly and in a different style, his attention wholly directed at her injury.

'We'll have to get those stairs carpeted so that

they're less slippery. You're always running round barefoot,' he said in his most prosaic comment yet.

Bunny feasted her eyes on his bent dark head, the gleam of the steel hoop in one ear, the line of his hard jaw, the perfection of his classic nose and wide sensual mouth. Butterflies flew in celebration in her stomach. The core at the heart of her pulsed and her heartbeat quickened. 'I missed you so much,' she said tensely. 'I'll marry you tomorrow if you want.'

'What?' Sebastian glanced up at her in bewilderment, his brain still visualising the potential damage to her foot. Brilliant dark-as-coal eyes assailed hers. *'Tomorrow?'*

Bunny winced because he wasn't making climbing down from her high horse any easier. 'I just meant that I'm happy to marry you whenever you like. I think I was sort of testing you before.'

Sebastian frowned. *'Testing* me?'

'I wanted you to love me before we got married but now I realise that that doesn't matter as much as I thought it did. It's how you treat me that counts and you treat me like I'm something precious.'

'Of course I do, because you *are!*' Sebastian stressed, pushing up his shirtsleeves one after another, strangely shy, now that it had come to crunch time, to say those words he had always sworn that he would never say. But she deserved those words because, even after all he'd said, she had been braver than he was and infinitely wiser when it came to such emotions to say them first. '*Obviously* I love you,' he framed in a driven undertone.

Bunny's beautiful green eyes opened very wide in shock but she deemed it words voiced out of kindness rather than truth, possibly even his attempt to ease the tension that had existed between them since his departure.

Sebastian walked away a few steps and then swung back. 'But how I felt wasn't obvious to me until Parker phoned and told me that you'd had an accident.'

'My goodness, why did he do that? It wasn't a serious fall. He shouldn't have bothered you.'

'*Bothered* me?' Sebastian repeated in disbelief. 'I expect to hear about any accident you have, no matter how minor. You're *my whole world*. If anything happened to you and our baby, I'd lose everything that makes life worth living.'

'I—I didn't realise I was that important to you,' Bunny stammered.

'And the bad news is that I didn't realise either until I was told you had had an accident and I was forced to spend some time thinking about that.' In front of her, Sebastian shuddered in remembrance. 'It was the worst thing that's ever happened to me... The very idea of losing you was unbearable. I couldn't handle it. It knocked me flat. I don't believe I spoke an intelligible word until I was halfway back here and your brother had calmed me down.'

'You spoke to John?' she gasped.

'I knew he was with you when it happened, so naturally I contacted him, assuming you'd be in hospital after the way Parker had spoken of the incident. It was a huge relief to learn that you were relatively unharmed, but I couldn't be content, I couldn't settle, until I saw you for myself,' he confided, approaching the bed to sink down beside her and wrap both arms around her. 'I'm so grateful that you're not badly hurt. I didn't think I could ever love anyone and then you came along.'

Conviction that he meant every word he was saying set into Bunny then and she relaxed for the first time in days. 'And annoyed the hell out of you at first glance.'

'No, I like your feisty side, the way you stand up to me. Very few people challenge me. You *did* and if you hadn't, I'd just have steamrollered over you because that's the way I'm built to react to challenges, so that's really positive for us as a couple,' he concluded.

'You love me,' Bunny recounted softly. 'And you know I love you.'

'Yes, and I was quite happy for you to love me even while I was telling you that I didn't believe in this kind of love,' he groaned. 'That was very selfish.'

'I was selfish too. I always wanted you to love me even though you said you couldn't. I set my heart on the *one* thing you'd told me you couldn't offer.'

'That's your stubborn backbone, but you were pushing me towards a cliff I needed to fall off…to find real happiness,' he breathed tautly. 'And I fell today the minute I had to face the concept of a life that didn't include you. It's good. Now we both know where we are…so you'd agree to marry me *tomorrow*? How did that timeline come about?'

Bunny went red, a little embarrassed even in the midst of that happiness to admit that she had felt kind of desperate and had feared that she was putting him through hoops because of the way Tristram had strung her along.

'I'm glad the little twerp did that if it means I got you instead!' Sebastian teased, not remotely concerned about anything she had done, lying back on the pillows to curve her close. 'Did I tell you that I checked him out and discovered that, far from being in finance as you assumed, Tristram is a podcaster?'

'A podcaster?' Bunny echoed in disbelief.

'Apparently he didn't do well in finance and he decided to interview minor celebrities instead. He's got a decent following but he's basically a paparazzo, which I assume explains why he was chasing after you.'

'He wanted the shipwreck story,' Bunny guessed and shook her head. 'I wouldn't have told him a word.'

The familiar scent of Sebastian flooded her as she buried her nose in his shirtfront and then he tipped up her face and his mouth closed over hers in an unashamedly hungry kiss. Her fancy outfit was tossed on the floor. Sebastian was far too busy telling her how beautiful she was and cupping the very faint swell of her belly with possessive enthusiasm to notice what she had worn. It wasn't very long until both of them were stripped and making passionate love. Bunny cried out his name in release and he groaned in ecstasy, cradling her against him when she was drowsy.

'It's a shame tomorrow would've been too short notice for your family,' Sebastian mused.

'What are you talking about?'

'Our wedding,' Sebastian told her with immense satisfaction. 'Do you think in two weeks' time?'

'You are so impatient,' she complained while hugging him with delight that he really couldn't wait to get that ring on her finger.

'I was scared of falling in love,' he admitted with startling abruptness. 'My father was obsessively jealous and possessive about my mother before she started the divorce and when I first began feeling weird about you I was afraid that his excessiveness might be in my DNA as well.'

'Weird?' Bunny queried. 'Weird about me?'

'Over-the-top possessive and not liking being without you. That's why I believed that, after our rescue, we should both spend some time apart,' he admitted.

'You spent our time apart organising this house for me,' she reminded him. 'How did that fit in?'

'It made me feel better to be making plans for us. I was miserable without you,' he confessed grudgingly.

'I was miserable too,' she whispered. 'And you're not the slightest bit obsessive or possessive. I like being with you too. It's normal when you're in love.'

'You always say the right thing,' Sebastian murmured, replete in his contentment.

In reality, it took Sebastian a whole month to get Bunny to the altar in her family's local church. Her wedding gown, hot off the fashion designer of the year's runway, made the front of many newspapers and several glossy magazines. Her dress was silk scattered with what were rumoured to be real diamonds. The hand-embroidered lace bodice defined her slender curves and then flowed down like some medieval princess gown. Her family surrounded her with Sebastian and it was the happiest day of her life. And *his*.

EPILOGUE

Five years later

'No, THREE CHILDREN is quite enough,' Bunny told her husband, eying four-year-old Argo, two-year-old Sofia and baby Will, named after Bunny's father.

Argo and Sofia were fighting over a toy and Sebastian was separating them while Will was crawling under the table in the great hall while Bunny completed the Christmas decorations for their party. 'Mum had five children only because she was desperate for a girl and I'm not a baby machine.'

'Won't mention it again,' Sebastian told her cheerfully, because Bunny was the broody one of the two of them and he was convinced that, once Will started running around, Bunny would decide on another.

Bunny grinned at him because she knew something he didn't as yet. And he would be over the moon because nobody loved kids more than Sebastian. Being on a high around Sebastian was anything but new to her. She felt like that most days, scrutinising his gorgeous face and tall, superb physique, still barely able to credit that he was hers. All hers, heart and soul and body, she thought fondly while a little skip of heat burned between her thighs.

Had it really been five years since their wedding? So much had changed since then but not the basics. They were still based at Knightsmead Court, although they enjoyed regular trips to other properties abroad. The house's library had quietly become famed among academics, who regularly called to request access to the ancient books and manuscripts that composed the original collection. It was a collection as well that was now being added to on a regular basis since Sebastian had come to appreciate how much his wife delighted in virtually running her own little academic library.

The year before, they had sailed in the yacht to Indonesia and had had a fabulous holiday. Andreas and Zoe and their children and Bunny's family had joined them. Now that the Greek couple were based in the UK again, Zoe had become Bunny's best friend. Andreas and Zoe also accompanied them to those chilly Pagonis gatherings, which Sebastian insisted should continue, and Bunny was beginning to see a definite defrosting of attitude from the younger generation of Sebastian's relatives. Old scandals and resentments had less of a hold on them than they had on his father's contemporaries in the family.

Her own family members were regular visitors. Indeed, Bunny had loved her husband even more when he'd begun to treat her family as if they were *his* own family, finding in them that warmth and affection and interest that he had long been denied by Loukia Pagonis's younger sons.

The children's nanny appeared to take the little ones up to bed and bath. Sebastian cornered his wife against the table. 'So what does that little secretive smile hide?' he asked, both arms firmly closed round her slender body.

Bunny ran her hands up over his splendid torso and slowly up to his shoulders, trying not to smile when she felt the quickening of his body against hers. Sebastian was always ready for de-stressing the natural way. 'Your super swimmers have already done it again. The shower last month when you...' her hands lifted to do little air quotes '...*forgot*. Our fourth is due in the autumn, by which time Will will be a toddler, so it's not a disaster except for my stretch marks.'

'What stretch marks?' he asked, because he only ever looked at her and saw his perfect woman, whom he adored, and as far as he was concerned she had no imperfections. She was the woman who had brought him alive, taught him to feel again and given him so much in the process: a true home, three fabulous children, endless loyalty and love.

'I love you,' she confided, kissing a path up his neck while dragging in the scent of his skin and the burn of her own arousal.

'I love you even more. You're the sun I revolve around,' he told her passionately as he lifted her onto the table, skilled fingers pushing her skirt out of the way.

The silence was slowly broken by little gasps and groans until finally they made themselves respectable again and he carried her over to an armchair to cradle her in possessive arms. 'I bet we have a girl next time.'

He was right but he was also wrong. The fourth pregnancy gave them twins, a boy called Christos and a girl called Annette after her maternal grandmother.

And they all lived happily ever after, in love, and positively boastful about their good fortune.

* * * * *

Did you fall in love with Shock Greek Heir?
*Then don't miss out on these other
intensely romantic stories from Lynne Graham!*

Two Secrets to Shock the Italian
Baby Worth Billions
Greek's Shotgun Wedding
Greek's One-Night Babies
His Royal Bride Replacement

Available Now!

HARLEQUIN
Reader Service

Enjoyed your book?

Try the perfect subscription for Romance readers and get more great books like this delivered right to your door.

See why over 10+ million readers have tried Harlequin Reader Service.

Start with a Free Welcome Collection with free books and a gift—valued over $20.

Choose any series in print or ebook.
See website for details and order today:

TryReaderService.com/subscriptions